THE PREQUEL TO THE RANFURLY MYSTERIES

INEVITABLE DANGER

K.M. KRENIK

KNOX
WORKS

Copy Editor: Jessica L. Powers
Proof Editor: Kim Beckham
Cover Design: 100 Covers
Interior Design: Miblart

Table of Contents

Acknowledgments

Thank you to my parents, my hubby, Robert, and my kids, Nathaniel, Keira, Lucas, and Bethany for inspiring the characters in the story.

Special thank you to my very talented and brilliant editors, Jessica Powers, copy editor, and Kim Beckham, proofread editor.

A shout out to my beta readers, who took the time to read and give me feedback on the chapters of the prequel: Rebecca Wer, Ali Simpson, Samantha Wallace, Sally Bryan, Koralyn Driskill, Abigail West. I hope you enjoy seeing how your input has made a difference. Your insight and encouragement spurred me on to make necessary changes and to keep moving forward with the story. Words can't express my gratitude.

Finally, many, many thanks to my readers, who are the inspiration for me to keep writing.

K.M.

A Word from the Author

This story takes place in a fantasy world. The timeline is not the future of our world.

CLIFF HANGER WARNING

In this prequel, mysteries are introduced. However, they are not solved by the end of this book. In fact, the end of the book is just the beginning, so prepare yourself to meet a cliff, and to hang there until book one of the series.

TRIGGER WARNING

Behind closed door sex scenes, mature, topics, alcohol use, violent situations. Parental discretion is advised.

 **1**

The question isn't whether or not danger will come,
but what will we do when it does?

COURTNEY

FUTURE - YEAR 2227
Mill Pond, Cascadia

"Stop! Please! Don't do this! Sto- Mmm! Mmm! Mm-Mm-Mmm!"

Duct tape was plastered over my mouth and my hands were being cuffed. Men in black business suits pointed their guns in my face.

"Get in, Blue Eyes," one of the men ordered, shoving the thick nose of his gun into my shoulder. I tried to climb into the SUV without the use of my hands, unsuccessfully. One of the men picked me up and practically threw me into the back seat. We drove a good hour until the driver pulled onto a private grass runway out in the middle of nowhere. A government plane with the words *PAX Eagle* was waiting for us.

The man in the front passenger seat of the SUV looked over his shoulder at me and said, "Time to fly." The driver got out and opened my door, and I hopped down to the ground. The men forced me to board the plane.

What were they going to do to me? I had no idea. I didn't want to let myself think about that. But what I couldn't stop thinking about was how I had messed up. Like a record on repeat, the thought went around and around in my head.

I had failed.

It was a simple enough mission, and I should have been able to carry it out. Now, people who I couldn't imagine living life without were going to die. And it was my fault.

The loud engine of the plane started up as one of the men told me to take a seat. He buckled me in, then plopped into a leather lounger that was across from me in the twelve-passenger jet. The seat would have been comfortable if I weren't cuffed and being held prisoner. The other man went a few rows in front of us and sat in a seat that had a table. We'd passed two pilots in the cockpit when we boarded, but other than that, we were the only three people on the plane. No flight attendant to pass out beverages, or to give instructions on what to do in case of a crash.

The window had a built-in dimmer, and was set all the way to "blackout" instead of having a shade to pull down. So, I didn't have a view of what was outside the plane. All I could see in the window was my own reflection, a disturbing picture with silver tape over my mouth. If my hands were free, I would have pressed the button that controlled the dimmer so I could look outside and get a clue as to where we might be headed.

The man across from me must have read my mind. "Have you ever heard of Site 205?" he sneered.

I crinkled my brow. He snickered. "Well, you're going to see it firsthand, soon enough."

I wondered if I was not really awake, but having a weird, long, life-like dream. Site 205 was a well-known government testing area, somewhere in The Desert Region, where they had God-only-knew-what hidden below the ground. Top secret stuff. But people knew about it, made up all sorts of stories about it. There were even movies about it. In fact, when I was a kid, one of my favorite cartoons had funky aliens who played in a rock band together and were always on the run from the government. The cartoon was called *Site 205*.

I rested my head back and closed my eyes. I needed to escape. Yea, you're probably thinking, escape! Be a hero. Amaze us with your brilliant plan of action! Uh no. Sorry. You have me mixed up with some other character. The one I wish I was. But I never set out to be a hero, never went looking for danger. My goal in life was to live a trouble-free, peaceful existence.

No, my way of escaping was in my mind.

Let's see, what can I think about? ...Meg. My mind often went back to Meg when I was dealing with a crises. Don't know why, it just did.

A time when life was simpler, when I was six years old, and the greatest worry was how to keep Meg's twin brother and his smelly friends out of our tree house.

FLASHBACK – AGE SIX
Meg's Tree House, The Goldens

"I know. Let's set up a bunch of booby traps!" my best friend Meg suggested.

"Okay! Like what?" I asked her.

"We could tie a bucket of water to a rope, place the trip trigger there," she pointed to the opening at the top of the tree house ladder, "and when Mikey comes up here with his friends, the first one of them that comes through will trip and get dumped on."

"But then everything will get wet in our tree house," I said.

"Oh. Right."

"But I like the way you're thinking. What other thing could we put in the bucket?" I asked.

"Hmm... I guess paint won't work either, " Meg said.

"Don't think so. Hmm. Is there anything stinky Mikey is scared of?" I asked.

She laughed. "Easy. Snakes. And our favorite cartoon, Site 205, because of the aliens."

"Oh! Well, we can fill it with fake snakes! The kind that feel real!" I said. "And hang up posters of the aliens all over inside."

She liked the idea. So, we begged her mom to take us to the local thrift store. We used our saved-up piggy bank money to buy a bunch of fake snakes and posters. The next time stinky Mikey and his two friends beat us to the tree house after school, and they usually did because they ran faster, we watched them climb the ladder... Mikey leading the way.

When her brother cried out and the boys came scrambling down the ladder and ran away screaming, we exchanged a look of pure satisfaction and gave each other a high five.

We painted a sign that said Site 205, and posted it outside the tree house. After that, Mikey and his buddies became suddenly disinterested in beating us to the tree house. Meg and I made the treehouse our home away from home.

LORD ROBERT

FLASHBACK – AGE SIX
Knoxfordshire Coast, The Green Isles

The beach was near Ranfurly Castle where he grew up. Six-year-old Robert walked with his mother, enjoying the feeling of tingly, wet sand under his toes.

"Do you hear the ocean?" his mother asked, holding a large, hollow seashell to his ear. Her eyes were gentle, hazel. Her hair was long, flowing, and golden, and her skin was a deep olive shade, because she came from the southern part of the mainland, La Belle Terre, where people had dark and beautiful complexions. "La mer," she said.

"La mer," Robert had repeated.

"Look mummy!" Leo, age five, looked just like his brother, the same bright green eyes, and dark, curly, almost black hair, like their father's. Their mother let their locks grow to their shoulders, because she couldn't bear to cut off those curls. Leo pulled on his mother's other hand. "Look at that!" He pointed to the ocean.

They watched as something massive with large, teal scales came up out of the water, then disappeared beneath the waves. The scales were smooth, like a snake's, and it moved like the body of an eel, but it's head never emerged. It was hard to tell how big the creature was, because the rest of its body remained hidden beneath the sea.

"What is it? A giant sea snake?" Leo asked.

His mother shook her head slowly. "Dragonne de la mer," she whispered.

"A Sea Dragon?" Little Robert looked out at the glassy, chartreuse combers where they had just seen the creature disappear below the surface. He'd only looked at pictures and heard stories of dragons in books. They stood and watched the breaking surf for a long time, hoping the creature would fully emerge so they could get a glimpse of its head.

"Have you ever seen a dragon before, Mummy?" Leo asked his mother.

"Only once before, when I was a little girl, not much older than you boys," she said quietly.

"What color was it?" Robert asked.

"It had orange scales, with many spikes on its back. Its body wasn't long like a Mer Dragon. It was shorter, with wings. A Flyer. Ah, I remember how beautiful the under-feathers were when it spread its wings wide. Shades of purple and blue, so magnifique. I looked up at the sky the rest of that day and for many days that followed, hoping to see the dragon again. People said it was good luck."

"Do you think we have good luck because we saw this dragon?" Leo asked.

"I hope so," their mother said. "But your father would say there is no such thing as luck, wouldn't he? He'd say we make our own luck. Perhaps he is right."

PRESENT – YEAR 2219
Upland Coast, The Green Isles

Lord Robert had been driving his motorbike along the Upland coast when the flashback came. He wondered why that memory had never been in his mind before. Something today had triggered it. He drove his bike to a lookout alongside the road, pulled off his helmet, and stared out at the ocean. "Hmm. Was that a real memory, or something I just conjured up?" he wondered. He hadn't heard about a dragon sighting in years. Dragons were considered endangered and the only place a person might spot one would be in on the island of Tanai. Thousands of miles away.

After watching the waves for a long time, Lord Robert recalled one more thing that happened, after they saw the dragon.

His mother let go of his and Leo's hands and ran into the ocean.

"No, mummy! Don't go in the ocean. The dragon might come back and take you!" Lord Robert had yelled and ran after her, into the huge waves. The waves had swallowed him up, and the next thing he remembered he was lying on the beach, with his mother holding him. Her golden hair fell like a curtain around his face.

"Little Rob Bear, you must learn to swim before you can go into the ocean," his mother said, her tears trickling onto his nose.

His beautiful, dark-skinned, golden-haired mother from La Belle Terre. He strained to remember more, but he couldn't.

The sound of his phone ringing shook Robert out of the memory. It was his friend, Raymond.

"The party started an hour ago. Are you coming or not?"

"Yes. On my way. Tell me you have something besides liquor. I'm famished."

"You know, these parties cost me a fortune. You ought to try throwing one sometime. I've got deviled eggs and other finger food, but if you don't get here soon, I can't promise there will be anything left."

"Deviled eggs?" Lord Robert scoffed. "I'll be there, after I stop off for a bite of something substantial. You know what my hangry side looks like."

"Hmm. Yes, I do. Not pretty. Make it quick, though," Raymond said. "There is someone here who is very anxious to see you," he sang the last part, teasing.

Lord Robert's stomach churned. He held back from saying the thing he desperately wanted to say, which was: "I'm actually feeling incredibly ill, Raymond. So sorry, I can't make it." Hunger pains swirled, intermixed with anxiety. He hated parties. But it was Raymond's birthday. He had to go to support his friend.

Lord Raymond Manfred was someone Robert had known since he was a boy, a third cousin. He was a count, the younger of two sons, and had studied law with Robert at the same university. But to the dismay of Raymond's father, he'd decided to become an actor.

Raymond's family was from the same area as Robert's, Knoxfordshire on The Green Isles, or The Greens, as some called it. It was an island region made up of The Highlands in the north, Knoxfordshire in the middle, and Upland in the south. The populated island was a three-hour boat ride off the main continent.

The main continent was historically divided into separate regions which were each ruled by monarchs: Bella La Terre, Gutland, Vinosa, Northland, and Portera, as well as The Green Isles. In recent years the monarchs made a treaty to merge under one currency in order to strengthen their economies, in hopes that tourism might flourish. They named the area Zone A. Across the ocean, the prosperous Democratic Republic continent of Chantelle caught on to the idea, and deemed their merged regions as Zone B. The rest of the continents soon followed. So it was that the regions of the globe were now separated into Zones.

Robert was from a long line of viscounts who governed Knoxfordshire, where Ranfurly Castle was situated. Like most noble houses, Robert and Raymond each owned a second residence in Upland, where the king resided and where the parliament met. After studying law at university, Robert took residence in his Upland House to work in parliament.

Lord Robert put his helmet back on and started his motorbike up. He took one last look out over the cliffs to admire the waves crashing into the rocks below, and gazed at the long span of vacant beach to the left of the cliffs. The familiar yearning was there again. An emptiness. More than just hunger pangs. He longed for what could never be.

He left the beach behind him and set off down the road. He inhaled the fresh sea air and sped up as he came to a long, downhill straightaway. The exhilarating ride was his way of shedding the stress after a long week of being cooped up writing bills, debating, and arguing with pig-headed parliament lords who were set in their ways.

He turned onto the road that headed inland, and caught sight of the ocean one last time in his rear-view mirror. The yearning returned as Robert wished he could see them again. Dragons. His mother. *Wishing. How pointless*. He'd learned that lesson years ago. Wishing only wounds the heart.

2

COURTNEY

FUTURE – YEAR 2227
In Flight

Hot flashes. Sweat. Shortened breaths. The urge to hurl. I had to fight it. Couldn't let those men see me freaking out. Couldn't puke on the plane. I wanted to be invisible. Like a lizard, I closed my eyes and hoped that if I couldn't see them, they wouldn't see me.

Come on, Courtney. You had two drug-free labors. You can do this. Breathe. In through the nose, slowly. Out through the nose, since my mouth was still taped shut. Cleansing breaths. *Think of happy thoughts. Something positive. Another memory... Lord Robert. Wait... no, not him. Think of Meg.* Sinking back in my seat, I heard a familiar voice.

My mother's voice calling me.

FLASHBACK – AGE SIXTEEN
Meg's Tree House

"Courtney! Where is she? We have to go!"

She was yelling from my backyard, and I was in the backyard next door, not wanting to answer her. We were moving away from my childhood home, away from my next-door neighbor and best friend Meg. Away from the tree house that knew all our secrets, watched us grow from the time we were six years old, through harrowing middle school, until that summer we'd both just turned sixteen.

Meg hugged me tightly, and through sobs said, "I'm not going to let them take you. You can just stay here with my family and live with us."

"Okay," I said. "I'll just stay here in the treehouse. We can ride motorcycles every day when you come home from school, and I'll survive on leftovers from your mom's cooking... that seafood chowder she makes practically every night." Her mom's chowder was disgusting. Bleh. We both laughed and I choked on snot mixed with tears. "Why don't we have any Kleenex in here? I'm a snotty mess!"

"So am I!" Meg said. "Here, you can blow your nose on me." She held out her T-shirt sleeve, and we both laughed through the disgusting slime coming out of our noses. "You should see your face right now, Crow. Brian Matthews would take one look at you and run!" Crow was the nickname she'd made up for me when we were in elementary school. My nickname for her was Mouse.

"Brian Matthews!" I busted up laughing. He'd been my crush when I was in kindergarten until third grade and had grown up to be the last guy I'd ever be interested in.

"I got blackmail proof right here, Crow." Meg pointed to the corner of the tree house where I had carved Courtney + Brian in the tree.

I sighed. "Promise me you'll never let your parents sell this place, Mouse. And never let them take down the tree house!"

"Okay. Should I make a blood pact with them?" Meg looked at me sideways with a half grin.

I laughed. "Yes! Oh, do you remember how freaked out I was when you made me prick my finger? The sight of blood!"

"You were always such a big wuss, Crow."

The nicknames were something we started when we were about eight years old. We'd often call each other with animal sounds outside. I got really good at mimicking crows, and Meg's impression of a mouse was spot on. She even freaked out her mom once, had her standing up on a chair with a broom, screaming, "Someone kill it! It's in this house somewhere. I heard it!"

Ah. Good times.

LORD ROBERT

PRESENT
On the Way to Raymond's House

He stopped off at his favorite chowder house and chomped down a hefty bowl of thick seafood chowder paired with freshly made sourdough bread smothered in loads of butter. He ordered a savory mug of warm ale which he took his nice, sweet time to drink. Afterward, he headed to Raymond's house, dreading that he had to go to the party the entire rest of his motorbike drive.

But it was Raymond's birthday, plus he'd won *Best Actor* in The Greens, a double celebration. He had to suck it up and go.

Raymond. Charming. Funny. Famous for portraying action heroes, warrior kings, and knights in films. Eyes of a deep brown that twinkled with mischief. Raymond his cousin, Raymond his buddy since childhood.

Robert didn't allow many people into his heart, but Raymond was an exception.

In addition to being a famous actor, Raymond had become known for throwing entertaining parties, which always included a large crowd of famous film stars and royals.

Robert knew the paparazzi would be there that night, as they always were. Unlike Raymond, who adored getting press, Robert preferred to avoid them. So, he walked up the boxwood-lined, cobblestone path that led to Raymond's two-story, brick house. He entered through the arched wooden doors, not bothering to knock. He never knocked at Raymond's house, and the butler knew Robert preferred no assistance when he came to visit.

Robert kept on his helmet, aware he probably looked out of place and a bit ridiculous. No doubt, a guy wearing all black leather and a motorbike helmet walking into the house was enough to turn some heads. But other than Raymond, the people at the party had no idea that it was Lord Robert Ranfurly under the helmet, and he reveled in his anonymity.

"I have no idea where he is, but he promised he'd be here," Raymond was saying to Lady Jane Monroe. They were standing right next to the entrance foyer, so Robert could hear them louder than everyone else in the noisy house.

Jane was a tall, gorgeous blond, who Robert had been seen publicly with a few times and now the rumor was that the two were an item. But in truth, Robert had no real interest in her.

Lady Jane was only twenty and was one of those people he kept at arms' distance. She was certainly a beauty with her soft, creamy complexion and lovely fair hair. But Robert preferred a motorcycle between his legs to a shiny, pretty ornament that took him nowhere, and would only attract even more attention to him.

The thing he hated most. Attention.

Just after Raymond finished speaking with Lady Jane and she wandered into the next room, the billiard room, Raymond spotted Robert standing in the foyer and made a beeline for him.

"Robert? What are you doing?" Raymond asked him in a low tone, out of earshot of his other guests.

"Observing from inside."

"From inside your helmet? Sometimes I wonder if you're severely mental."

"Look, you know I don't want to be followed around by the press. And I really don't want to see Lady Jane right now," Robert said.

"Can't you just get over your antisocial behaviors for one night? For my sake? It means a lot to me, you know, that you're here. God knows my own family would never come to a party with a herd of actors. You're the closest thing to family I've got."

Robert sighed. "Actually, I *am* family, Raymond. Your third cousin, remember? And you're right. I'm acting like a selfish prick. Happy birthday. And congratulations." Robert pulled out an envelope. "For you."

"Thank you, my man. You didn't have to."

"It isn't much," Robert dismissed.

Raymond opened the card and pulled out two tickets to his and Robert's favorite martial arts fighting event of the year. "The Vigilantes! Yes! The Green Isles team will be competing in it this year. Oh, what?! You managed to get us a box seat!"

"Yes. And it will be held in the ancient coliseum in Vinosa this year. We can stay in my villa there."

Raymond hugged his friend. "You truly are the best, mate. Thank you. Means the world."

"You deserve it. Well, I suppose I should head upstairs to change," Lord Robert said.

"Yes, your tux is in my bedroom hanging up for you, as you requested," Raymond said. "I'll keep Lady Jane company until you get back."

A hush came over the room. A woman walked in through the front doors. Flaming red locks flowing down to her waist attracted everyone's attention. Raymond's butler appeared instantly at her service.

"Oh look, everyone!" Raymond said, as the woman waited for the butler to take her fur shawl off her shoulders. "My glorious co-star, the warrior princess, has arrived, fashionably late as always!" Raymond announced. Everyone applauded and cheered. Lord Robert had seen the film, and had heard plenty of stories about the actress, who'd been deemed the title, *Sexiest Woman Alive*. But he'd never met her.

It wasn't a surprise to Robert that she'd earned the title. She was a juicy thing, he thought, watching her. The way she swayed her hips when she walked, it was enough to bring on a feeling of hazy intoxication. She made her way over to a pair of men who were looking at her as if she were a piece of juicy steak they were eager to sink their teeth into.

He turned to head upstairs, but then he heard her laugh. A rich, throaty laugh, that made him stop and turn to look at her once more. She was animatedly engaged in conversation with the flock of men that had gathered around her. Something about her voice, her plump, red-painted lips moving as she spoke, was hypnotizing.

He forgot his original plan to head upstairs as his eyes drank in the rest of her. She wore an emerald-studded, floor-length, silk dress that clung to her hourglass figure, and a center slit to the top of her thighs revealed the shapely, muscular legs of a dancer. Those crimson flames of hair combined with very lively blue eyes seemed to emanate sparks. Sparks that ignited something inside him he'd never felt.

"You haven't met my bewitching co-star yet, have you?" Raymond said quietly to Lord Robert, watching him, somehow aware that underneath the helmet, Robert's eyes were glued to Desiree.

"No, I haven't," Robert said. Something about being called out like that by Raymond sobered him up from his temporal state of intoxication. He watched the way every man in the room flocked around Desiree, the way she seemed to adore all the attention, and shook himself, as if he could flick his thoughts off of him like he would flick an insect.

"Yes, Clark!" She was telling one of the men. "I literally just got off the phone with the director and found out I got the lead in *The Mermaid*!" She squealed in delight and grabbed hands with the man named Clark. They jumped up and down like a pair of happy elves.

"Desiree, congratulations!" Raymond cut into the group of men. "So glad you made the party tonight."

"Raymond, love! Congratulations to you. Best Actor! I'm not at all surprised. And happy birthday." Desiree kissed him passionately on the lips. For some reason, Robert felt uncomfortable and looked away, focusing on the art deco styled portraits on the walls. But he'd seen Raymond's modern décor a million times, and there was nothing else in the room of interest, so he looked back to continue watching Raymond and Desiree, who were now laughing, nose to nose.

Desiree's eyes flickered around the room, taking in the guests. Then she noticed him, and he stared into her eyes, forgetting he was still wearing his helmet. Like the rest of the guests, she had no idea who he was.

"Mmm. Who's the mystery motor biker? Is he an entertainer?" she asked Raymond, appraising Lord Robert's muscular frame.

Raymond laughed. "You would have liked that, wouldn't you, my dear?" He kissed her hand. "No, he isn't here to do a strip tease. But..." Raymond's eyes flashed over at Lord Robert and a wicked grin crossed his face. He spoke loudly, so the whole room could hear. "Our disguised guest will be revealed later this evening. There will be an award for anyone who can guess correctly who the man in the helmet is."

"Oh! What fun!" Desiree clapped with glee. "Who could it be? Perhaps he will give us a little clue? Take off his jacket to let us see what is underneath?"

Lord Robert shook his head slowly.

"Sorry, but this one keeps all of his clothes on, Desiree. Even his jacket. No clues, no hints," laughed Raymond.

Lord Robert gave a nod to Desiree, and saluted the rest of the room, before he bounded upstairs and darted into Raymond's bedroom, where he, at last, took refuge. He let out his breath through flapping lips. Alone, at last. Something about a room full of people always brought on anxiety. Raymond's bedroom was like a sanctuary that he had no desire to leave. He'd avoid going downstairs to face the party crowd for as long as possible.

Like the rest of the house, Raymond's bedroom was in the art deco style, with a walnut bed that had carvings of a phoenix in the head frame, and a huge picture hung on the wall over the bed. It was from one of the films Raymond had starred in, and portrayed Raymond in a jungle, wearing a brown leather jacket, a khaki shirt and pants, a brown outback fedora hat, and carrying a whip over his shoulder. He had his arm around a tiger. That was the film that made Raymond famous, where he and his pet tiger shared many jungle adventures.

Robert took off his helmet, pulled off the biker habit, and changed into the tux that the butler had hung up for him in Raymond's bedroom. For some reason, Raymond made his guests dress up in tuxedos at his house parties. Robert thought it was a little unnecessary, but Raymond and his actor friends were funny.

Leaving his shoes off, he propped down in a dark green velour chair, where he got lost in phone texts and emails. When he finished that, he skimmed through the latest news. Forty minutes had passed when Raymond finally barged into the room.

"What are you still doing in here? I thought you would have come out by now. The guests are all asking who the man in the helmet is. Especially Desiree."

"Desiree. She seems to like all the attention, doesn't she?" Robert rolled his eyes.

"Ah, yes." Raymond meowed like a tiger. "Desiree. Mmm, what a woman. I mean, Lady Jane is amazing and all. A perfect picture of high-class nobility, that one. But Desiree... well, the woman is on *fire*. And it's like she has some sort of power over men. You felt it, didn't you?"

Lord Robert shrugged. "Not really. She seems a bit... over the top."

Raymond raised an eyebrow. "What is with you? Why can't you just relax and have a little more fun in life, my man? Seriously, if I were you, I'd be showing off that gorgeous, flowing mane of yours, instead of wearing it in an uptight little man bun. Why not try enjoying all the attention people give you, instead of always hiding from it?"

"I hate the attention. But I must admit, I do have good hair," he joked.

"Good hair. I'll say. I hate you for it, especially since mine is beginning to recede. Talk about making a person feel old. So, are you going to come out of my bedroom, or do you plan to stay in here and read the news all night?"

"Yes. Fine. Fine." Robert got up reluctantly and started to follow Raymond down the stairs.

"Wait. Actually," Raymond held up a hand to indicate to Robert he needed to stop. "Wait here until I announce you," he ordered. Robert froze in place, outside the bedroom doors, which were out of sight of the downstairs. Raymond ran halfway down the stairwell, stopping on the center landing, where the room below had a clear view of him. The center landing was large, a perfect platform for an actor who loved a stage.

"Ladies and Gentlemen!" Raymond announced in a strong, well-seasoned baritone. "Remember our mystery guest? Did everyone write their guesses down and put them in the box in the foyer? If you haven't, do it now. In five minutes, I will announce who the mystery man in the motorbike helmet is!"

The crowd buzzed with excitement and scrimmaged to find the pads and pens in the room so they could write down their guesses. Once the room had settled down, Raymond made his anticipated announcement.

"Desiree, my leading lady, will you grab the box of guesses and bring it up here? Then come on up here and help me read them, and we'll see whether or not we have a winner."

Desiree glided through the room with the box, and climbed the steps to the center landing, taking her place next to Raymond. The couple began pulling the little pieces of papers out of the box, one by one, reading off the guesses. Once finished, Raymond said, "Unbelievable! You've *all* been duped! Not even *one* of you guessed correctly."

The crowd yelled out, "Boo!" and asked each other, "Who can it be?" "Did you think it was Jack?" "I thought for sure it was Gregory!" "No, I was certain it was that model we used for our last film!" "I thought it was the stunt man on Runaway Wheels!" And etc...

Desiree dramatically grabbed Raymond by the throat. "Raymond! You can't keep your guests waiting any longer! You are *killing* us with curiosity. We must know who this mystery man is!"

Raymond laughed and said, "Very well. I suppose I don't want to gain a reputation as the man who *killed* everyone at his party. So, I shall announce who the mystery man is, before you curious kittens all fall over and die. Drum roll please..."

Some of the people in the crowd started hitting glasses and tapping their feet on the floor.

"Ladies and Gentlemen... the mystery man of the evening is..." Raymond looked around the room, then pretended to die. The room gasped and booed.

"You dirty rat! How dare you torture us by dying before you tell us!" Desiree ran down the steps and grabbed a glass of bubbly out of a random person's hand, ran back up the steps, and poured it on Raymond. He was instantly resurrected.

"Revived by good spirits!" he cried. Everyone cheered and hollered.

"Mystery guest! Mystery guest!" The room was now chanting and yelling.

"What's that? You want to know who the mystery guest is? Oh yes. I almost forgot. Caught up in heaven and all that."

"Hmm. You in heaven? That seems highly questionable," Desiree said with a smirk.

"And the mystery guest of the evening is.... Lord Robert Ranfurly!"

The room was silent. This was clearly a surprise. Everyone knew very well who Lord Robert Ranfurly was, Upland's Most Eligible Bachelor. The best looking, wealthiest man in The Greens. But he was also the most mysterious, most untouchable, a man who never went to parties. How did Raymond manage to get him to come to this party? They all wondered. Then they began clapping. Cheering.

Lord Robert desperately wanted to retreat back into Raymond's bedroom, and would have liked to strangle his friend at that moment. *"Here, all I wanted was to remain anonymous,"* he thought as he walked down the steps slowly, guests hooting, whistling, and hollering.

Wearing a black tuxedo, hair pulled back into a man bun, the way he always wore it, the women in the room swooned. He approached the center landing in the middle of the stairway, where Desiree's lively pale blue eyes devoured him.

"Well," she said in her sexy voice, "what a surprise this is! Lord Robert Ranfurly. You grace us with your presence. I've heard so much about you, I feel like I know you already." She held out a hand for him to kiss. Robert took her fingers in his but didn't kiss the hand.

"Really? What exactly have you heard?" he asked her.

"Oh, you know. Lord Robert, The Viscount of Knoxfordshire, Upland's Most Eligible Bachelor who will never settle down," she moved in closer and whispered the next part into his ear. "Not even the breathtaking Lady Jane is good enough for him." A corner of her lip curled up. "Some even claim you must have a distaste for women." Desiree gave him a sideways glance.

"Is that right? Well, I might have heard a few things about you, as well," Lord Robert said in a low tone.

"Really? What have you heard about me?" A coy smile crossed Desiree's face.

"I couldn't possibly repeat it. That would be spreading scandalous gossip, wouldn't it?"

She laughed. "You wicked! But, really, Lord Robert, it is curious that a man as devilishly handsome as you hasn't been snatched up yet." Desiree playfully put a hand on Robert's chest.

"Perhaps I haven't found anyone who is my type," Lord Robert said, unflinching at her touch.

"Really? And what *is* your type, exactly? Since rumor has it that you aren't really into Lady Jane. Is that true?" Desiree moved in and pressed up against him, her lips nearly touching his. She stayed there, waiting for him to do what all men did, return her advances.

Instead, Lord Robert turned his head slightly so that his lips brushed against her ear. He whispered, "I find subtlety and discretion extremely sexy in a woman, but sadly these days those qualities are nearly impossible to find. And as for Lady Jane and me, well, as I already mentioned, I'm not a fan of scandalous gossip." Lord Robert stepped back, putting a distance between them, and said in a casual way, "Well, I must say, Ms. Diamond, to meet you has been... *something*. Now, if you'll excuse me."

At that, he continued his descent down the steps, leaving Desiree to gape after him. He walked over to Lady Jane, who had been watching his every move with admiration and worship. Desiree stood frozen, shocked. She'd met some really arrogant people in her line of work. But Lord Robert had to be at the top of the list of most arrogant men she'd ever met.

3

COURTNEY

FLASHBACK – AGE SIXTEEN
Meg's Tree House

"Hey, Courtney? Meg? Girls, I'm sorry, but you need to say goodbye. Courtney has to go," Meg's dad called up to us from below the tree house. "Her parents have to meet the realtor at the house in Cascadia before five o'clock tonight, and they have a twelve-hour drive to get there."

I looked at Meg and made a sad puppy face.

"Too bad your parents don't have one of those new hover cars. You'd get there a lot faster." Meg squeezed me one last time and handed me a peacock feather.

"What's this?" I asked her.

"A parting gift. I found it yesterday, when I was walking by that acreage where they have all those noisy peacocks," she said, tapping me on the nose with the feather and handing it to me before we climbed down the ladder.

As we pulled out of our driveway in The Goldens, and drove off in our van, I looked out the window and waved goodbye to Meg, her twin brother Mikey, (who we'd come to get along with since high school), and their parents. I held tightly to the peacock feather. The next day, while unpacking and decorating my room in my new house in Cascadia, I put the feather in a jar.

The feather was still in that same jar, sitting on a shelf in my family room back in Mill Pond.

LORD ROBERT

PRESENT
Upland

After Raymond's party, Desiree got revenge on Lord Robert for slighting her. If Lord Robert's name came up in a conversation, she made a point to let people know her opinion of the man.

"Oh, please. Don't let that gorgeous face fool you. The man is a peacock without a soul," she told the press once when they asked if she would ever date him. The press lapped up her insult like it was a delicious treat, and they fortified her opinion by expounding upon it with juicier words. The slander earned Lord Robert a new nickname: *Most Eligible Peacock.*

A month later, Lord Robert was at home in his Upland house when his butler came into the study and announced, "Lady Jane is here to see you, Sir."

Robert sighed. He sat at a large mahogany desk, surrounded by walls covered with mahogany shelves filled with hard-covered books. Robert faced a computer monitor, papers were spread out all across the desk, and he was looking over more papers that he held in his hand. "I'm right in the middle of looking over this bill. Can you tell her I'm ill?"

"She says it is urgent, Your Lordship."

Lord Robert stared at the butler with a raised eyebrow. Well-practiced in serving nobility, the butler remained expressionless.

"Fine. Fine." Lord Robert set the papers he was holding down. "I know what you're thinking, even though you'll never admit it. You think I'm being an arse."

"I certainly would not have said that Your Lordship," the butler said.

"No. You wouldn't. But you thought it, none the less." Robert got up from his desk. "Show her into the parlor, I'll meet her in there."

A few minutes later, he greeted Lady Jane in his parlor. It had high ceilings and huge windows on each side of a walk-in fireplace, which at the moment had a fire lit in it. The mantle was painted navy, and above the fireplace hung a painted portrait of Robert's parents. A brown leather couch and a pair of navy velvet chairs were placed in the center of the room around a mahogany octagon-shaped coffee table.

Lady Jane was standing next to the fireplace, looking perplexed; not the usual, pristine, poised flower he was used to seeing.

"Have you been crying? What is it? Has something happened to your parents? Your sister?"

An annoyed look crossed her face. "No. No, nothing has happened to my family. Something much worse is bothering me and I was hoping you could help."

"What's going on?" Lord Robert was alarmed. He'd never seen Lady Jane act so strangely before.

"Well, I- Do you know Prince Jakobe?"

"From the mainland? The North Region? Yes. He's a distant cousin, somewhere down the line, I think. Although our looks would never give that away, them being albinos and my family line having darker features."

"Mmhmm. He proposed to me last night," Lady Jane said flatly.

Lord Robert laughed at the thought. Prince Jakobe had to be twenty-five years her senior. It was normal for royal men to marry much younger women, but he knew Lady Jane could find a more suitable match if she waited a little longer.

"You find that funny?" Lady Jane's face fell like a deflated balloon.

"Well- I mean... surely you're not thinking of marrying him?"

"Lord Robert, he's a prince. With a wealthy territory to rule, and he will rule, because he is the only son. That means he'll be a king, which would make me a future queen. So, yes. I'm thinking about marrying him."

"But he is old enough to be your father. And you are so young and beautiful. You really could do better than that. The north is freezing in the winter, not a very comfortable climate to be a queen of."

"Well, I'll work on my designs when it is freezing out," Lady Jane said. "Besides, I'm not a fan of the outdoors, anyway."

"Your designs?" Robert asked.

"Yes. I want to have my own fashion line," she said.

"Oh. I had no idea."

"Probably because you never asked. And it isn't as if I have any other proposals waiting for me. Is it?" She looked at Robert, hope in her eyes.

"Well, I mean, you're how old? Twenty? You have plenty of time to find someone who you might actually have feelings for."

Lady Jane withered like a flower into a parlor chair.

"Everyone assumed you and I were going to end up together, so all my other possibilities have already moved on. In fact, they're already married. That's why, if you aren't planning to propose, I'm going to have to marry Prince Jakobe." With a look of hopeful desperation, she batted her eyes at him, a helpless kitten.

"I'm so sorry, Lady Jane, if I have misled you. But in truth, I have no intentions of ever marrying." He paused, then thought he should probably say something more. Grabbing one of her tiny, delicate hands, he noticed the ink-stained fingertips, most likely due to her working on her designs, he thought. He'd never even asked her about her interests. Didn't know she had any. At that moment, perhaps out of guilt, he was more sincere than he'd ever been with her. "I truly wish you all happiness with Prince Jakobe if this is what you choose. And success as a designer."

Lady Jane stared at him for a moment, as if in shock. Then, as the truth seemed to light up in her head, she stood slowly, trying to maintain her dignity and poise. It was evident to Lord Robert that he had crushed the young woman. She'd made it obvious that she worshipped him. But he couldn't return her feelings, no matter how much effort he gave it. Still, he felt like a rat.

"You know, you are so lovely, if only I were the type to want to settle down... I'd choose you among any other woman." That part wasn't true. "I do hope you don't rush into marrying someone for the sake of a title, Lady Jane. Wait for the right one, he'll come along." That part was true.

Lord Robert tried his best to comfort her, but he watched the withering flower leave Upland House that day with petals falling off of her.

TWO YEARS LATER...

The feeling of guilt eventually wore off after breaking the young woman's heart. Robert got more involved in his work, and was living the glorious life of a recluse. Two years flew by. Robert was sometimes asked to teach seminars in The Capital City across the ocean, in Zone B. Whenever he went there, his other closest friend, Peter Williams, who'd been one of his professors in law school, invited him to stay at his home. Peter was a Justice, and his wife Nina was a reform counselor for ex-criminals.

Peter and Nina lived on a quiet street lined with sugar maples just outside the center of The Capital City. It was away from the high crime areas and the noisy parts of town. Their two-story house, painted white, with pillars on the front porch that supported a large balcony over the black, double-door entrance, looked like a miniature replica of where the President of Zone B resided.

"Still living the bachelor life, Robert?" Nina asked him, as they sat around their dining table after one of her delicious home-cooked meals.

Robert nodded. "I'm afraid Peter snatched up the best woman on the planet. Can't find anyone who compares to you."

Nina laughed. "Oh, my! Flatterer!"

"Hey, no trying to steal her from me, Robert. But you're right. My wife is the best woman on the planet. And she makes the best fried chicken in the world. Mmm. Lovin' this sauce, babe." Peter licked his fingers after taking a bite out of a chicken leg.

"What can I say? I'm finger-lickin' good." Nina's cocoa skin was a tad lighter than her husband's. She was tall, lean, and fit, thanks to her addiction to running. Peter had been in great shape back when Robert met him in Upland. But on this particular visit, Robert noticed Peter was getting a little soft.

"You better be careful, Peter. Your wife's cooking is catching up with your waistline," Robert teased.

"Hey! I resemble that comment," Peter scowled.

"He's right, babe. You need to get your lazy butt out of bed in the mornings and go for runs with me. Don't want my killer sauce killin' my man." Peter made a puppy face, and Nina laughed. She leaned over and gave him a kiss on the cheek. "But my love for you is unconditional," she sang to him.

"I don't deserve you," Peter said. The pair laughed, and Robert felt a twinge of envy.

Nina had an uncanny way of seeming to read people's minds. She looked at Robert and said, "You know, I'm going to keep praying the right woman comes along for you, Robert."

Robert laughed. "You can save your prayers for more important things. I'm not looking for a woman."

Nina lifted her eyebrows, a twinkle in her deep brown eyes. "No? Well, Peter wasn't looking for a woman when I met him either."

"She's right. I wasn't." Peter took another bite of his juicy chicken that was smothered in Nina's special sauce. "But God had better plans for this ole boy."

The couple laughed again, looking into each other's eyes. Robert watched them in admiration. What those two had was other-worldly. Not possible for the majority of people to find. Nina was Peter's match in every way, his partner, his friend, his lover. She was strong, opinionated, wise.

Robert could never imagine finding someone who would be his match. No point even wishing for it.

"Oh, I have something for dessert too. Be right back!" Nina got up and went through a swinging door into the kitchen, then a moment later came back with a birthday cake, candles lit. "Happy birthday to you. Happy birthday to you," Nina sang in a rich, low alto voice. Peter joined her in his raspy baritone, singing, "Happy birthday, Lord Robert. Happy birthday to you!"

"Wow. You two remembered it was my birthday." Robert laughed. "And I was hoping to skip aging this year. That cake looks amazing!"

"It's chocolate whipped frosting, white cake, and raspberry filling. Your favorite, right?" Nina asked.

"Maybe I should just move in with you two, so I can share your wife, Peter," Robert joked. "Seriously, thank you. This is so... unexpected. And kind."

"You're family, Robert," Peter said. Nina nodded.

"That's right." Nina nodded. "And who knows? This might be the year you finally meet the right woman."

Robert arrived back in Upland, and at the airport he bumped into Raymond.

"Woah! Fancy running into you here, mate!" Raymond said.

"You look tan. Is that from a bottle?" Robert asked.

"No, it's real. I just got back from filming over in The Tropics. Did some lounging around by the hotel pool on my days off."

"Livin' the dream," Robert said.

"Always. Only way to live!" Raymond patted Robert on the back, nearly knocking the wind out of him. "Speaking of living, wasn't yesterday your birthday?" Raymond asked.

"Mmm. Was it?" Robert hated remembering it.

"Yes, indeed, it was. Alright, then. If I remember right, your favorite fish restaurant is on the way home, and surely you're starved after the long flight? I certainly am."

"You're not wrong about that. Sounds like a good deal to me."

Robert swallowed down a buttery, creamy bite of white fish with pasta, then took a sip of wine. "Thanks for the birthday dinner, Raymond. Although I keep trying to forget I'm having another birthday."

"No problem, so lucky we bumped into each other. By the way, have you seen *The Mermaid* yet? It just came out. I went to the opening show with Desiree, and she was stunning in it. Oh. Wait. I forgot. You don't care much for my friend, Desiree, do you?"

"What? I have no feelings any which way about her, whatsoever. And no, I haven't had time to watch movies."

"Oh. I know Desiree has said some terrible things about you, though. Thought the feeling might be mutual."

Robert made a frown. "Nope. I never listen to what anyone has to say about me. Especially if it is written in the press."

"You know she is dating Wellington, right?"

Robert nearly choked on his next bite. "As in August Wellington? The not-noble noble?"

Raymond laughed. "What, because he bought his nobility? Is that why you call him that?"

"It has a double meaning, Raymond. The man is crooked. All around. And buying a title is like screaming out from the rooftops that a person is desperate to climb a social ladder, don't you think?"

"What I think of titles and all the rest... pompous nonsense. Besides, with the way things are changing, it will soon all be ancient history," Raymond said.

"What are you talking about?" Robert was confused.

Raymond clicked his tongue. "Robert, Robert, Robert. You think you know so much because you work in parliament. But as an actor, I travel the world, attend parties, and play golf with many interesting people. Some of those people are in powerful places. I hear a lot of things."

"Such as?"

"One word you should know. Globalists."

"Globalists are a bunch of childish billionaires who believe they can create a utopia, Raymond."

"They aren't all childish. I happen to know one at the top of the chain. And he told me they have plans, Robert, interesting plans. Plans that will strip monarchies of power. Kings and queens will be nothing more than symbolic heads. Zone B will change, as well. It already *is* changing. The people there will believe they are still a democracy, but the globalist leaders will make sure whoever runs that side of the world is too stupid to think for themselves. The administration they have now is already proof that the globalists are accomplishing their goal. We're next."

"Who is this globalist you've been talking to?" Robert asked Raymond.

"A billionaire, and a genius. He's going to oversee global media. And in my field, getting to know him is the most important thing an actor can do for their career. Anyway, my point is, your title, and mine, will soon mean nothing."

"How soon does your friend think this global takeover will happen?"

"He didn't give a date, but he said it will happen subtly. People won't realize anything has changed while the takeover is happening right under their noses. Which, of course, means it could be happening as we speak."

"That's alarming, don't you think?" Robert asked Raymond.

Raymond shrugged. "As long as I have a good job, a good life, get paid, I have no complaints. Plus, I've always thought titles to be pretentious, anyway, so I'll be fine when all of that dissolves."

Raymond and Robert had a nice time, went to see *The Mermaid*, which Robert thought had a ridiculous plot, but when Desiree was on screen he didn't care about the plot. In the film she portrayed a topless, singing mermaid, and her long red hair covered her breasts in a way that teased. Her singing voice was also fantastic, a voice critics raved about, and the haunting song she sang in the film was beautiful. *Who needs a good plot when Desiree is the star of a movie?* Robert thought on their way back to his Upland house.

The following week, Raymond flew off to film another movie while Robert went back to being a recluse.

Since *The Mermaid* film came out, web posts about Desiree Diamond were the most read news in all of The Green Isles. "The dazzling Diamond, notorious for breaking men's hearts, now has her clutches in Bad Boy Wellington."

Robert was lying in his four-poster mahogany bed one morning, reading the news, when he saw the posts about Desiree and August. He cringed. August Wellington, who showed up to parliament on occasion because it made him look important, and the rest of the time dabbled in film acting. Cheated his way through university. Insulted people who had no title. Even though he had to buy his own. The man wasn't even born in Zone A. He was from The Goldens, in Zone B, a democracy. *Pretentious prick.*

Lord Robert looked at a social media photo of the couple that had gone viral. He thought to himself, "Ridiculous name mashup. Augiree! Pff! What an unlikely couple they make." He scowled at the photo. August wore the same thin-lipped, smug smirk on his face as always, and looked like a beige wall standing next to the gorgeous beauty with flaming red hair.

"What does a woman like her see in a pancake like Wellington?" Robert's stomach churned.

Wellington. Always wore the most expensive suits, shoes, cologne. Bleached white hair, usually slicked back with too much gel. Neatly trimmed beard formed into a twirly point at his chin. Robert could easily envision two horns poking out of the man's head and a pitchfork in his hand.

The man was an elitist who loved to look and smell rich. But vanity wasn't his worst trait. The fact that he treated the lower class as if they were inferior. No. He treated everyone as if they were inferior. That was his worst trait.

"Pff! Most Eligible Peacock," Lord Robert muttered to himself. "If ever there was a person deserving of that title, she's dating him now."

A few days after Lord Robert saw the photo of the couple, he was meeting some business colleagues for dinner at an exclusive club in Upland when August and Desiree, (Augiree) walked in and sat at a nearby table. Robert found himself stealing glances their way, not because he gave a rip about August. But Desiree was so enchanting that it was difficult to peel his eyes away from her. At one point, Desiree caught him staring at her, and she gave him an icy glare in return.

Later that evening, Robert left his colleagues to head home, and on his way to his car he heard a man yelling. He noticed Lord August's sporty motorcar parked nearby, in an empty side lot, and realized the yelling had come from that direction. In Robert's clear view from where he stood, August and Desiree were having a spat.

"You really had to gamble everything, August?"

"You stupid @#*!" August spewed at Desiree, then backhanded her across the face. "What I do with my money is my business! Now, get in the car!"

Robert saw Desiree cup her hand over her face, where she'd been hit. Wellington grabbed her by the wrists, and drug her into the car, slamming the door on her once she was inside.

Robert's reaction was to intervene. He ran toward them, not thinking about what he was going to do, only that he had to act. But by the time he'd reached them, Lord August had already screeched out of the parking lot.

A few days went by, and Robert couldn't get the scene out of his mind, nor could he stop thinking about Desiree. Why would a woman as beautiful, as sought after as she was, settle for someone like August? She could have had any man she wanted.

"What could I possibly do to stop that monster?" Robert asked himself. *"Talking to him wouldn't be helpful, that was certain. But perhaps a warning. Hmm."*

The next day, Robert saw August at parliament, and overheard him speaking with another lord.

"Right, I'll see you tonight at the club, then. Do you want to use sabre or foil for our match?"

"Ah, my foil is damaged. Let's use sabre," the other man said to August.

"Hmm. He's going to be at the fencing club tonight. Good," thought Robert.

Robert also belonged to the fencing club, and went there after work almost every night to train and sometimes compete in matches. That evening, after work, he went home to change into his fencing uniform. He had all of his own equipment, but he kept it at home, not in the locker at the club. He'd invested far too much in his weapons and uniform to risk leaving it in a locker.

He grabbed his sabre belt and sabre, then headed to the fencing club. Once at the club, he put on his belt, sabre in its sheath, and entered. He walked past the different studios where fencers were engaged in matches. At last, he came to the studio where Lord August was in a match with someone.

Once August's opponent left the room, Robert entered. August was alone. It was the perfect moment to say what he wanted to say.

"August," Robert said, purposely omitting the title. August was busy messing with his fencing helmet, and jumped a bit when he saw Lord Robert.

"Yes?" August asked in his condescending way.

"May I have a word with you?"

A look of curiosity crossed August's face. "I suppose."

"I saw you the other night at the restaurant when you were by your car with Desiree Diamond. The way you backhanded her across her face. I wonder how Desiree's face looks after that hit? You know, you're lucky I didn't catch up to you that night. God knows what I might have done."

"How... How dare you!" Lord August said, turning red.

"It takes the smallest, most cowardly of men to hit a woman. You've proven to me that's exactly what you are. Nothing but a tiny, little coward of a man."

"Excuse me? Who do you...what are you even doing in here?" August stammered. "How dare you come in here, into *my* club and hurl insults at me like that. And as for Desiree, she despises you. And the woman is mine... my business. You'd be wise to stay out of my business." August raised his sabre that he was still holding after the match.

Robert's sabre was still in a sheath on his belt, within a second's reach. "Is that a threat, August?" Robert felt his face get hotter, as he glared at August.

August was a couple inches shorter than Robert, and lifted his chin, nostrils flaring. "We're done here." He stormed out of the room.

"Hurt her again, you'll answer to me, August," Robert called after him.

August didn't look back. Robert took a few breaths, cooled down, and went into a different studio, where another club member was going to meet him for a match. While he waited for his opponent to show, Robert got out aggression on a training dummy, imagining August's twisted smirk and devilish head on it. Finally, the club member he'd waited for arrived, and they engaged in a few practice matches. An hour later they finished, and Robert put his sabre back in the sheath on his belt and headed out to his car.

August was waiting for him by his car, sabre in hand.

"How dare you approach me inside the club and insult me like that," August's top lip curled up in a sneer. The red neon lights on a nearby sign reflected in his eyes, making him appear even more like a devil. "Did you expect me to do nothing? Lord Robert Ranfurly. Viscount of Knoxfordshire. You've always thought you were so much better than me, because of your title and rank. Now you're just jealous because I have something you and every other man wants."

"Please, spare me. I don't want anything you have. Oh. And if you're talking about Desiree, hate to break it to you, sport, but a woman isn't a *possession*."

"You're lecturing me on women?" August laughed. "You? I know for a fact that you're pathetic when it comes to how to treat a woman. I heard it firsthand from Melinda Rose Buchanan. Remember her? From university? She came crying to me when you broke her little heart."

"Well, at least Melinda was smart enough to figure out quickly that you weren't worthy of her. I was happy to see her marry someone who was a real gentleman. With a *real* title."

August's face grew red. "Why don't we discuss this like two *real* men?" August pointed his sabre at Robert's chest.

"Very well," Robert's sabre was still in its sheath. He quickly jumped back from August's blade, but August lunged at Robert, and sliced him in the arm.

"I've learned a few tricks since the last time you faced me in a fencing match," August spewed.

"Tricks? Is that what you call attacking an unarmed opponent? A trick?" Robert said, ignoring the gash and the blood that began to spill out of it. Instead, he used the distraction of their dialogue to reach into his sheath and pulled out his own sabre, then lunged toward August. August just escaped the lunge as he ran around the car and put a barrier between them.

"I'm not surprised at all that you play dirty," Robert continued. "A man who cheated his way through university, who *bought* his title. Perhaps

that is what is at the root of your abusive nature? An inferiority complex."
Robert's words sent August into an outrage, and he came around the car
full force, aiming for the lung.

Robert saw him coming and jumped to the side, slicing into August's
fencing hand. Sabre dropped to the ground. Blood spurted everywhere.
August cried out in pain.

"Better take care of that hand, August," Robert said. August picked
up his sabre with his other hand and ran back into the club.

"Stay away from me, Robert!" August yelled as he was running off.

LORD ROBERT

PRESENT
Upland House

Robert couldn't get Desiree off of his mind. *"What if by confronting August, I just poked a stick at a snake? He might be even more abusive toward her. I'd hate myself if I brought on even more distress for her."* For the next few days, he tossed and turned at night, trying to come up with a way to get Desiree to stop seeing August.

At last, an idea came to him. An idea he hated, but his own sacrifice and discomfort was worth it, if it meant saving Desiree from further harm. He called his friend Raymond.

"Raymond, you know how you often say I'm letting the Upland House go to waste by never hosting parties here? Well, I've decided you're right. I'm going to throw a holiday party this year, and I'd like to invite you and your friends to be my guests of honor."

"Wait. Is this really Robert? As in Lord Robert Ranfurly? My friend, and cousin, who is antisocial and hates parties?"

"Yes, it is me. I know. Out of character. But, I've been working far too much, and... well, maybe I need a change."

"I think I'm actually speechless, Robert," Raymond said.

"Not possible," Robert said.

"I can't believe it. I've always thought your mansion would be an amazing place to have a party."

"Can you help me get ready for it? I'm not the most experienced at throwing parties, as you know."

"Of course, I'll help!" Raymond exclaimed. "I have a few friends who love to decorate. Leave the games up to me. And I know the best caterer. You did say you were paying for all of that, didn't you?"

Lord Robert laughed. "Did I? I was thinking you could front the bill," he teased.

Raymond laughed. "I'm still paying off the last party I threw. Your party, your bill, mate."

"Right. Suppose so. Will you also make sure to get the word out to everyone?" Lord Robert asked him.

"Certainly. But wait. Do you mean everyone, everyone?" Raymond asked. "Or should I not mention it to my friend Desiree? I know you two have a reputation for being Upland's arch enemies."

"Nonsense. Raymond, I told you I have nothing against her. In fact, I'd be honored to have her come to the party."

"Excellent! I'll be sure to let her know she is invited, then." Raymond paused. "And Lord August? I know he's always been an annoying prick, but they are together, after all."

Robert clenched his fists. Of course, he didn't want to invite August into his home. But he didn't want to risk Desiree not coming because he overlooked her boyfriend. "Don't send him an invitation, but if that's who Desiree brings as her plus one, then so be it."

The party was the following weekend, and all the rage. Everyone from the acting community, and then some, showed up for it. The only person who didn't show was the one Lord Robert threw the party to see. *Desiree.*

"Where is she?" he wondered. *"She certainly doesn't seem the type to skip a party. After two years, the woman is still holding a grudge against me."* Robert shook his head, frustrated.

Two hours later, Robert had given up on seeing Desiree, when she was announced at the front door by the butler. Dressed in the finest Caleb di Bianco dress, white silk, with gold stilettos, and a beaded gold handbag hung by a string of pearls from her forearm. Her dress accentuated all of the enticing curves and lines of her delicious figure. Ringlets of crimson cascaded her remarkable high cheekbones and diamond-shaped face. Every eye in the room was on her, as she scanned over their faces with her long-lashed pale blue eyes. When she saw Lord Robert standing across the room staring at her, she met his gaze. Lord Robert crossed the room to greet her.

"Thank you for accepting my invitation, Ms. Diamond," Robert said to her, warmly.

"You have quite an exquisite home, here, Lord Robert," Desiree said, not warmly.

"Did you come alone this evening?" he asked her, hoping she did. He searched her face, and noticed the excessive powder. He saw the faint discoloration under her eye. She was covering up a bruise, no doubt.

A second after the words came out of his mouth, to Robert's deep dissatisfaction, Lord August came in behind Desiree and wrapped his arms around her waist. Robert noticed one of August's hands, the one he'd slashed in their fight, was in a cast. "Come along, my love," he said to Desiree. The pair crossed the room to mingle with a cluster of actors by the grand piano.

"*Someone needs a refresher in proper manners,*" Lord Robert thought, thinking of how much he'd like to teach August another lesson with a sharper sabre.

Robert's plan was to approach Desiree when she was alone at the party, away from the crowded room, away from August. He had to wait far longer than he liked for the opportunity. Then, at last, Robert noticed her slip upstairs to the water closet. He glanced around, and saw Lord August was in the billiard room, in the middle of a game. No other guests were upstairs, so he grabbed a glass of cherry bubbly and casually made his way to the second floor. He stood in the hall, next to the water closet.

The woman took her nice, sweet time inside the restroom. At last, she came out of the water closet, and Lord Robert "accidentally" ran into her. The bright red beverage in his hand spilled all over her gorgeous, white dress.

"Oh, no! My brand new di Bianco dress!" she cried.

"Oh, I'm terribly sorry. How clumsy of me," Lord Robert said, sincerely. "Please forgive me, Ms. Diamond."

"Well, it would be forgivable if this dress hadn't cost me my entire month's earnings!"

"I'm sorry. Really. Please, let me make it up to you," he pleaded.

"No, it's fine," she snapped. "There's nothing to be done about it." She started to head down the stairs.

"I know Caleb di Bianco personally. I can introduce you to him." Lord Robert said.

Desiree stopped and turned around. She studied Lord Robert's face, trying to discern whether or not he was joking. Robert went on. "You know, come to think of it, Caleb has mentioned to me before that he would love to create a dress for you. You wear everything so very well."

Desiree laughed. "You're terrible. Stop teasing me, you monster."

"I'm not teasing," Lord Robert said earnestly. "I'm quite serious." He gently put a hand on her arm, his emerald eyes rested on Desiree's lips, and he felt her lose her balance. He pulled her away from the top of the stairs. "Be careful not to fall, Ms. Diamond."

"Wellington would be furious with me if he saw me speaking with you," she whispered, glancing downstairs, looking for him. "He despises you."

"I assure you; my feelings for him are quite mutual. But you are a strong, independent woman, Desiree. Do you honestly care what he thinks?" Lord Robert challenged her.

Desiree smiled, and a look of defiance came across her face. "I should very much like to meet Caleb di Bianco. When can you arrange it?"

Robert pulled out his cell phone and sent a text. "Let's see. I just sent Caleb a message asking him when he'll be available. May I have your number? I'll let you know as soon as I hear from him."

"I suppose so," Desiree said. Lord Robert handed her his phone, and she tapped her number into it, then handed it back. A second later his phone dinged.

"Oh, we're in luck," Robert said. "It's Caleb. He replied. Hmm. He has an opening tomorrow, at nine o'clock in the morning. Will that work, Ms. Diamond?"

Desiree made a face. "Ew. So early?"

"We are talking about Caleb di Bianco, here," Robert raised a brow.

She laughed and shrugged. "You're right. He's worth getting up for, isn't he? Alright, then. It's a date, Lord Robert."

"Shall I come pick you up, then, and drive you to Caleb's office?"

Desiree looked behind her and scanned the room below. August could be partially seen in the billiard room, still wrapped up in his game. She turned back to Robert and quietly told him her address. Robert typed it into his phone.

The next morning, Lord Robert picked Desiree up on his motorbike.

"Really? I wasn't expecting to have to get on the back of that," Desiree scowled.

"No? Have you never ridden on a motorbike before?" he asked her.

"Actually, yes. I have. But certainly, never this early in the morning, and I'm not at all dressed to ride."

"So, go change. I can wait a few minutes."

Desiree huffed and headed back into her townhouse, while Robert waited out on his bike. She came out in tight black leather pants, a leather jacket, and thigh-high, red boots with spiked heels. Robert had to catch his breath, as she walked out with swinging hips, her gorgeous crimson locks falling down to her waist.

He handed her a helmet and watched her in admiration as she put it on. When she hoisted her legs over the seat behind him, he enjoyed the feeling of her pressing up against him, and wrapping her arms tightly around his waist.

They rode to Caleb's office, which was on the second floor of a six-hundred-year-old stone building in downtown Upland. There wasn't an elevator, so they climbed the steep stone steps to the second floor, and knocked on the brightly painted yellow door to his office. A petite blond answered the door.

"Come in. We're ready for you!" she said in a Bellaise accent.

Robert had been to Caleb's office several times, but he enjoyed watching Desiree's reaction when they entered the waiting room. A fireplace with a spectacular mantle was the focal point, made of pure gold, with designs of dragons in it, one colorized in red rubies, one in orange topaz, and the center dragon was designed in white alexandrite.

"Oh my! That is spectacular. I've never seen anything like it. Is the gold real?"

The woman nodded. "And so are the stones. Caleb's family crest is the dragon," the woman said.

"The white dragon. And our family stone is alexandrite," Caleb said. "I'm Caleb di Bianco, and I see you've met my wife, Emilie. We already know who you are, Ms. Diamond. Pleasure to meet you, at last."

"The pleasure is all mine, I assure you!" Desiree beamed. Robert enjoyed watching the sheer thrill written across her beautiful face, and he couldn't wait to spring his next surprise on her. "And the alexandrite stone is my June birthstone."

Caleb invited them to follow him through a royal blue door that opened to the next room. A large, bright room, with huge windows, several mannequins dressed in Caleb's designs. In the center of the room was a platform where he and Emilie took measurements and fitted their models. An orange settee faced the platform, and a huge mirror was on a wall to the right. To the left was a purple door that led to a private dressing room, and next to it was a large easel, covered by a white cloth.

Time to spring the next surprise, thought Robert. "Caleb, would it be possible for you to design three dresses instead of just one for Ms. Diamond?" he asked.

Caleb's mouth hit the floor. Desiree gasped.

"I think that Caleb is trying to say yes," Emilie said, laughing at her husband. Caleb's reaction had something to do with the fact that Lord Robert paid top, top dollar for his work. Not to mention, Robert was his number one favorite client.

As Emilie took Desiree's measurements, the actress said, "I feel like I'm on top of the moon!"

"Just wait!" Emilie said. "You will be transported to new galaxies in my husband's designs."

"I already sketched the first design, Ms. Diamond." Caleb pulled up the cloth that was concealing a large sketch pad on the easel. "What do you think?"

She bit her fingernails, excited. "Oh! Mr. di Bianco! You're truly a master mind."

"Call me Caleb. Please."

Caleb, originally from The Goldens, wasn't the type of man who looked like he spent a lot of time indoors, designing dresses. He was tall, muscular and broad-shouldered, and on his wall hung trophies he'd won in global martial arts championships. Yet, as unlikely as it seemed, this man was a world renown designer.

Robert met Caleb when he was in the martial arts scene before he broke into the high fashion industry. Back then, he was known for his designs for martial arts fighters. Caleb's first love had been science, which was why his uniforms were so exceptional. He incorporated his knowledge into his designs, and was able to offer fighters protection that no other clothing designer was capable of. His designs often had secret compartments and other surprises as well.

Robert had subscribed to everything di Bianco long ago, before Caleb became famous, knowing full well there wasn't another designer in the world who held a candle to him. Eventually, his talent became world known. Then he met Emilie, and she convinced him to add high fashion designs to his repertoire. Turned out he was incredible at that too. His high fashion designs were timeless, classic, yet always had Caleb's modern scientific elements that made the clothing line not only great looking, but comfortable and suitable for the environment in which they were worn.

"Ms. Diamond!" Emilie cried in excitement. "What an amazing coincidence. Your measurements are perfect for a dress we already have here!" Emilie cried. "It isn't spoken for yet. Caleb designed it with a model in mind for our upcoming show. Would you like to try it on?"

"Oh! Yes! Please!"

A few minutes later, Desiree came out of the dressing room and modeled Caleb's design. She looked as smashing as ever in a forest green, off the shoulder dress, with a wraparound skirt. An alexandrite dragon emblem was used to attach each off-the-shoulder sleeve to the bodice.

"It was like it was made for you all along!" cried Emilie.

"Oh my, Ms. Diamond," Caleb reveled. "I would love you to model this dress at the show. If you would do me the honor, the dress will be yours at no cost."

The look Desiree gave Robert could have sent *him* to another galaxy. He enjoyed the sensation of pure elation, something he hadn't felt since... come to think of it, he'd never felt that way before.

"You look irresistible, Ms. Diamond," Robert said, with no exaggeration. He'd been sitting in an orange loveseat, unable to strip his eyes away from her.

Desiree's cheeks turned a deep shade of pink. Robert wondered, *"Have I actually managed to make her blush?"* The thought of doing so delighted him. "Have I earned your forgiveness?" he asked her, in earshot of Caleb and Emilie.

Caleb looked at Lord Robert with a raised brow. "Emilie, come with me for a moment. I need to show you something in the other room. Excuse us," Caleb said to Robert and Desiree, as he took Emilie by the hand and left the room.

Desiree laughed. "Really, Lord Robert. You are quite surprising. Here, I thought we were supposed to be enemies, and now you're treating me like royalty. Why the change of heart? Was it really just because you ruined my dress?"

Lord Robert didn't tell her it was because he'd seen a different side of her that night in the parking lot when she'd been smacked in the face by her brute boyfriend. He didn't tell her how he longed to whisk her far away from Lord August. Instead, he told her something that wasn't untrue. "I suppose I've come to realize you are quite possibly the most interesting woman I've ever laid eyes on. And I'd very much like to get to know you better. If that's alright with you?"

"You do know I'm already spoken for? Lord August has practically proposed to me," Desiree lifted her chin.

"But he hasn't, though, has he? And you haven't accepted any proposals, have you?" Robert asked, a half-smile came over his face.

Desiree let out a long sigh. She shook her head.

"And I'm almost certain that Lord August would not be able to pay Caleb to design you a dress, would he?" Robert smirked.

"Shame on you, Lord Robert. That is not a very tactful thing to say," Desiree scolded.

"True. That was low of me." He got up and took her hand. "I suppose that means I need to earn your forgiveness again now. For saying that. If I buy you lunch after this, will you forgive me?"

"Well. I could eat an elephant right about now. I'm famished."

"Better not. I don't think Caleb's dresses will fit so well if you stuff down an elephant," Lord Robert teased.

They spent the entire day together. Lunch. A ride along the coast. Dinner at Robert's favorite chowder house. As they spent more time together, Robert saw a side to Desiree he didn't expect.

Beneath the powdered complexion, was an unadorned soul. A child-like girl. The way she ran, laughed, she reminded him of someone. A carefree child with red hair and freckles. A girl he once knew.

FLASHBACK – AGE NINE
Knoxfordshire Castle, The Green Isles

After their mother died, their father left Leo and Robert in their nanny's care, but sometimes their nanny became preoccupied with other responsibilities, and let the boys play a long time outside, unsupervised. During that unsupervised time, the boys manage to dig a hole underneath the castle wall and crawled through it to the other side, where there was a village.

In the village, they had all sorts of adventures. Some of their most interesting adventures began when they met a little red-headed girl who was living with her father on the streets. She often ran around alone. Her father taught her how to pick pockets and steal. Told her it was her "job." She was younger than the boys, probably six or seven.

"I double dog dare you to take that man's sandwich when he isn't looking." The very first time Leo and Robert met the girl, she'd challenged them.

"No. That's stealing. Don't you know it isn't right to steal?" Nine-year-old Robert told the little girl.

"It is not stealing! It is my occupation!" She said.

"What's a occupation?" Leo asked.

"An occupation is a job, Leo. But stealing is not a job. It is a crime. The Crown puts people who steal in prison." Robert folded his arms, imitating his father, and turned to the girl. "Why don't you go to school like other kids your age?"

The girl laughed. "I don't have to go to school! Unlike you, I already have a job! And I won't go to prison because I'll never get caught. Besides, I steal from rich people, and my father and I are poor and hungry. This is how we survive, so it isn't wrong for us to do it."

"I'll get the sandwich for you, if you're hungry," said Leo, ignoring Robert.

"Thank you Leo. You're much nicer than your mean brother," the girl stuck out her tongue at Robert.

Leo took the man's sandwich, and the little girl and Leo ran off and hid somewhere. Robert stood by the table, and was still frowning after them when the man returned.

"Where's my sandwich?" the man bellowed.

Robert's eyes grew large, and he stared at the man, frightened.

"You! You took my sandwich, didn't you, kid?"

Robert shook his head slowly, afraid to speak. The man glared at him. "I should report you to the authorities. But I'm feeling soft today. Go on. Get out of here, before I change my mind."

Robert was furious with his brother and that little girl. But the next day, Leo ran off to play with the girl again, so Robert went along with his brother to look after him. Make sure he was safe. That day, the three of them found a creek and pretended to run from pirates. They became friends after that, but Robert always reprimanded the girl when she stole things. And she always claimed that she wasn't doing anything wrong. Just doing her job.

PRESENT
Upland

What was that little girl's name? Katie? Kitty? He couldn't remember. *I wonder whatever happened to her?* he thought. They played with her for a couple of years, until Robert was around eleven, and that girl was probably around nine years old. But then one day Leo and Robert never saw her on the streets anymore. He'd often wondered whether she finally got caught and was taken to a prison for juveniles.

Something about Desiree... was it her laugh? Her freckles and red hair? The obstinate look in her pale blue eyes? Something about her reminded him of that little girl.

That same evening of Caleb's fitting, after a full day together, they finally stood on Desiree's front porch of her townhouse, and Robert had the strangest feelings of longing. Hunger. He wanted more time with the infectious creature. As she was about to close the front door of her townhouse, he asked, "Can we do this again sometime?"

"I'd like that," Desiree said, a coy smile came to her lips. Lips he would very much like to kiss. But it was far too soon for that. He could wait.

The next evening, he picked her up on his motorbike. Then, the next evening, in his sports car. Which she liked. A lot. The evening after that, he picked her up again in the same sports car.

Everywhere they went, paparazzi lurked in the shadows with their cameras ready, hoping to catch a perfect shot of the pair engaged in red hot acts. But Robert was patient. He never tried to kiss Desiree, or make a move on her, and he was so absorbed in her company he was unaware of anyone else around.

Even so, the press knew how to doctor up a photo, and the pair had given them plenty of footage and camera angles to play with. The best shot was when Lord Robert chased Desiree on the beach and once he caught her, they crashed onto the sand, him on top of her. That one was gold in their hands.

Two days later, social media stories had exploded over the latest news about Desiree Diamond and Lord Robert. Stories went viral. The name mashup the press came up with for the couple: "Desiree + Robert = Dessert. Yummy yum!"

COURTNEY

FLASHBACK – AGE SIXTEEN
Mill Pond, Cascadia

Every school has mean girls, and Mill Pond High was no exception. I figured out real fast who the mean girls were at my new high school.

Through the cracks, I saw them, two platinum blonds in cheerleading outfits putting on makeup. I'll refer to them as Blond 1 and Blond 2.

Blond 1: "She thinks she's all that on her purple motorcycle."

Blond 2: "And she was so rude to me; she rode her nasty motorcycle through a puddle yesterday and it splashed all over my new outfit."

Blond 1: "What a #@*!"

Blond 2: "She didn't even have the audacity to say she was sorry. Typical snob who thinks she's better than us because she's from The Goldens. I'm so sick of people from The Goldens moving up here and bringing their city ways. My father says they're ruining our town."

I rolled my eyes. City ways. She was the one with the fake hair, nails, and tan.

Blond 1: "I heard a couple people say they think Keith Drake is into her. Does that bother you?"

Blond 2: "Oh please. People are saying that? Keith is not into her. I asked him, and he says he thinks she is butt ugly. Besides, he's never been into brunettes. He's told me a million times how much he loves that I'm blond." The mean girls giggled and applied more makeup to their already overly done faces.

It was my third day at a brand-new high school. Mill Pond High was a small school, only about two hundred students, and they all seemed to know each other. In fact, most of them were related.

But I didn't know anyone. I had no idea who Keith Drake was yet. I didn't even know the girls who were talking dirt about me in the bathroom.

It wasn't easy to come from The Goldens and move to that small town. I had a reputation because of where I came from. Everyone assumed people from The Goldens were city slickers, obsessed with materialism, and that we looked down on rural people.

They were wrong about me being materialistic. The only possessions I cared about were my motorcycle, my music collections, and my books. I didn't wear makeup, didn't buy designer brands, didn't dress up nice.

But I guess they weren't wrong about the fact that I was a city slicker. I preferred the city, where there were things to do besides chew tobacco and log evergreen trees.

And maybe they weren't even wrong about me looking down on them. I certainly didn't care one iota for the people I'd met so far at Mill Pond High, and if someone would have given me a ticket out of there, I wouldn't have thought twice about jetting back to The Goldens and living in Meg's tree house.

It was my parents' knuckle-brain idea to move away from The Goldens. I never wanted to. Sure, Mill Pond was a pretty area. Pretty trees. Mountains. Rivers. Yada yada. But there was nothing to do. No music stores or dance studios where I could get quality lessons.

The high school had a gun club, a horse-back riding club, and a hiking club. I was never into sports, and even if I were, the only options at the school were volleyball, soccer, and baseball. Or I could join the cheer squad, which at the time, I was determined to never do. Not for me.

My parents would have to drive me thirty minutes away for opportunities that used to be in walking distance from my house.

I hated that little town, and pretty much checked out for the first month after moving there. My existence became: go to school, ignore everyone, go home, sleep. Rinse and repeat. Until about a month after school started, when I went to my first music lesson in the city thirty minutes away. Mr. Lyons' Music Studio.

From the outside, the building looked like it was about to fall over. But then, once you were inside, the walls were covered in guitars, ukuleles, basses, violins, cellos, and the floor displayed keyboards, drums, wind, brass instruments, even a harp. A smaller adjacent room held a section of music books. The aroma of wood from the guitars mixed with new book smell filled the place. And there was always a faint hint of tobacco. The kind that Mr. Lyons put in his pipe, which he sometimes smoked in the back room.

A wing of the building was dedicated to lessons, and there were about ten small studios with pianos in them, large enough for a teacher and maybe two students maximum to fit in. Every studio was decorated uniquely, each had a genre theme of its own.

I took a seat in a boho chair that was in the little waiting area for students. Someone was also waiting for a lesson, but I didn't look at them. Feeling shy, I avoided eye contact and looked out the window.

"*Are these yours? They fell out of your folder.*" The person who I'd tried to not look at was leaning toward me, reaching out to hand me music books I'd dropped. I looked into the face of the most gorgeous guy I'd ever laid eyes on.

"*Oh! Yes. Thank you,*" I cleared my voice, finding it difficult to act normal. I took my books from him.

"*You're the new girl from The Goldens, right? I go to Mill Pond High too. You're in my Bellais class. My name in the class is Pierre. Yours is Alicia, right?*"

I felt my cheeks flush. "*Um. That's the name I use in class because it is a Bellais name, but my real name is Courtney. Courtney Lane.*"

He nodded. "*You ride a motorcycle, right?*"

"*Yea. Why? Do you ride?*"

"*I drive a pickup, for now. But I like to ride dirt bikes around my property.*"

"*Oh, sounds fun.*" I smiled, bit my lip, and looked out the window at my motorcycle. I wondered what I must look like. No doubt, my hair was a long, windblown mess. I absently combed my hand through it and noticed he was watching me in the reflection of the window. He had blue eyes. Beautiful, grey-blue eyes.

"*I take piano. What about you?*" He asked, addressing my reflection.

"*Um, singing lessons.*" I looked over at him and smiled, not knowing what else to say.

Gorgeous Guy Pierre kept glancing my way and smiling at me. I shifted in my seat, feeling awkward, and hoped I wasn't slouching or looking stupid somehow. Finally, Mr. Lyons popped his head out of his studio and said, "*Ah, you're here. Come in.*"

I got up to go into my lesson, and Gorgeous Guy Pierre got up at the same time. We bumped into each other.

"*Oh, sorry about that!*" he said. "*Are you okay?*"

"*No, I'm sorry. Yes, I'm fine,*" I laughed.

"Wait, did you think it was your lesson time or something?" He looked at me, confused.

"Um, well. Yea," I said, worried I'd gotten my time wrong.

"This has been my lesson time for three years," he said. I felt awful. Had I messed up the time? Or the day?

He looked at me and said reassuringly, "Well, don't worry. Let's check with Mr. Lyons to find out. I bet he made a mistake or something." He smiled and indicated for me to go ahead. "Ladies first."

We went into the small studio. It had a piano, a mirror, a couple of chairs and music stands, and the genre it was designed to fit was the Animaniac 2100s. During that time in history, bands painted their faces to look like animals and incorporated animal sounds into their music. Recently, it had made a huge comeback. Nothing new under the sun, they say.

"Have a seat at the piano," Mr. Lyons instructed Gorgeous Guy Pierre. "And Courtney, you stand there."

"Mr. Lyons, I'm confused. This is my lesson time, right?" Gorgeous Guy Pierre asked.

"Yes. And it is Courtney's lesson time, as well," the music teacher said.

"But... these are supposed to be private lessons," Gorgeous Guy Pierre said slowly, not without respect.

Mr. Lyons sighed. "You have been taking piano lessons for three years now. Yes?"

"Yes," Gorgeous Guy Pierre answered. I noticed how dark and long his eyelashes were. Why did guys always get beautiful eyelashes?

"Why?" Mr. Lyons asked him.

"Um... why? Why what?" Gorgeous Guy Pierre asked, confused.

"Why do you take piano? Is it because you like to hear yourself play?"

"Uh..." Gorgeous Guy Pierre shifted in the piano seat uncomfortably. "Not really."

"No? Then why? Why do you want to learn to play piano? What are you going to do with knowing how to play?"

"I don't know." Gorgeous Guy Pierre was the one blushing now, and I felt horrible for him. I'd only met Mr. Lyons once at the audition when I tried out to be his student. But seeing the way he treated Gorgeous Guy, Mr. Lyons seemed kind of cruel.

Mr. Lyons looked at me. "This young lady has a good voice. Much potential. I want her to sing a solo in the upcoming recital. But she needs an accompanist. Have you ever accompanied a singer, Mr. Drake?"

"No, sir." Gorgeous Guy Pierre – Mr. Drake – said.

"Well, you are going to accompany Courtney Lane on the piano when she sings her solo. This is why, for now, you must share your lesson time, Keith."

I froze. Keith. Mr. Drake. Keith Drake.

"Is this okay with you Ms. Lane?" Mr. Lyons asked me.

"Uh, yea. Okay," I said, awkward. Keith Drake. I was cornered in a small music room with the hottest guy in school, Keith Drake. The same Keith Drake who apparently preferred blonds, and thought I was butt ugly. I tried not to have a panic attack and found myself wishing I had my best friend with me.

Keith stumbled through the intro to the song, and I came in at the proper measure. He stopped playing and turned his head to look at me when he heard my voice.

"Oh my... wow. Mr. Lyons, you ain't lyin'. She can really sing. I'm so sorry that I don't know the song well yet. I promise I'll get better for you," he said that last part directly to me.

"Hmph. Perhaps you will practice more now, Mr. Drake. Work together, both of you. I'll be back in twenty minutes." Mr. Lyons left us alone to practice.

Gorgeous Guy Pierre was actually Mean Guy Keith Drake who thought I was butt ugly. And now I was trapped in a tiny room alone with him for thirty minutes.

"You know, I've been wanting to get to know you for a while now," Keith said.

"Really? That's not what I heard," I said, no longer feeling shy, but irritated with him and his snotty crowd.

"What do you mean? What did you hear?"

"I heard you thought I was butt ugly. And something was mentioned about how you don't care for brunettes."

"What? That's crazy. I never said that. Ever." He laughed. "Don't believe what anyone says around here. Where did you hear that anyway?"

"Oh, from a certain pair of platinum blonds with fake tans who are obsessed with working out and getting their nails done. One of them seems to have staked her claim on you," I said.

"Oh. You mean J.C. I just broke up with her. Don't believe a word she says. And for the record, I never said you were butt ugly."

"Oh really. Not even to appease your jealous girlfriend?"

Keith looked at me sideways, and I squinted and glared back at him. He laughed.

"Wow. Okay. Fine. Maybe I did say it to appease her," he admitted. "But maybe that's because she was right to be jealous. Ask any guy, they'll say you're the most beautiful girl in Cascadia."

"Oh, please! I'd bet money on it that the guys around here haven't seen much outside of the tiny town of Mill Pond."

Keith laughed. "I guess that's true. Most of them haven't. But I have. I've been all over Cascadia, to The Goldens, The Capital Region, even to La Belle Terre. And I haven't seen a girl that compares to you in any of those places."

I felt my cheeks get suddenly warm. "Pff. Sweet talk will get you nowhere with me. You're right. I can't believe anything anyone around here says. Including you." I laughed and punched him in the shoulder.

After the lesson, while riding my motorcycle the thirty minutes back to Mill Pond, my spirits were elevated.

6

LORD ROBERT

PRESENT
Upland

"Is it the Final Farewell to Augiree?" The social media post sent Lord August Wellington raging like a rabid animal foaming at the mouth.

Robert forgot August existed. How could he forget that when August was an abusive threat to Desiree? You might ask. It's a fair question. But, as Raymond had once said, Desiree had a strange power over men. The power to make a man forget everything else. To only think of her.

Robert was no exception. His waking thought was to see Desiree, to spend every last minute with her. At night he obsessed about her.

After a few weeks of shamelessly spending time with Desiree, missing work to spend time with her, she suddenly stopped answering his calls.

Her latest film was on location locally, so he stopped by the set to see if he could catch her there. That's when he learned that they'd halted filming because Desiree had been out sick.

At that point, Lord Robert became concerned. He went to her small, attached townhouse, which he'd often dropped her off at, but never gone inside of. Three steps and a small landing led to her front door. Robert rapped at the door persistently, but she didn't answer. "Desiree, it's Robert. I've been worried about you. Please, if you're here, let me see you."

A nosy lady in the attached townhouse next door peered out their window at him. He waved to her. "Checking on my friend here, making sure she's alright. Have you seen her come out of her house?" he shouted to her. She shut her blinds.

Desiree's door didn't have a dead bolt. He pulled out his pocketknife and picked her lock. The front door opened easily.

"Too easily," he thought to himself. He searched every room in her house. It wasn't a large place, but it was decorated in boho patterns, colorful scarves hung over tables, beads hung between the kitchen and living area, plants hung all over, and it smelled like a strong, earthy incense. The downstairs had an open floor plan with a kitchen, eating area, and living room. He went upstairs and looked into one bedroom. It had a desk, bookshelves, a table with a sewing machine, costumes hanging up, and mannequin heads wearing wigs. He opened the closet to find nothing but several more costumes.

Next, he headed into the hall bathroom. She wasn't there. The last room to check was the final bedroom upstairs. The door was cracked open. He went in slowly. "Desiree? It's me Robert. Are you in here?" She wasn't in her room. He noticed the closet door cracked open, and he could have sworn he saw it move. He walked over to the closet and opened it. She wasn't inside.

"Where is she?" He checked her hall closet, nothing but shelves with linens.

He headed back downstairs, but swore he heard the floor creak above him. Was it coming from the sewing room? He went back up into the sewing room, and saw the closet door was more open than how he'd left it. He went to look in and pulled the costumes back. He then realized that a giant donkey head moved slightly. He pulled the head up and there was Desiree, staring at him. She screamed when she saw him.

"Desiree! What are you doing?" Robert asked her.

"Lord Robert! I heard someone break into my house, and was scared out of my mind, so I hid in here."

"You didn't hear me knocking on your front door? Calling out to you in your house? I was worried sick about you." Lord Robert then noticed her bruised face. "Dear God. August did this to you, didn't he?"

Desiree didn't reply, but stood still, silent. He pulled her in and held her. She was shaking. He held her until he felt her relax in his arms. Stroking her beautiful, crimson locks, he whispered, "Why do you settle for a monster like Wellington. Why?"

Desiree looked up at him, and Robert saw the little girl behind the woman's blue eyes. A girl who needed his protection. He closed the gap between them and pressed her into him. He would never allow anyone to hurt her again. He gently kissed her bruises, then eventually his lips found their way to hers. His strength and powerful passion overwhelmed her, and she became weak in his arms. Heat rose inside him as he kissed her harder.

The viscount had never before experienced that consuming fire of being obsessively in love. For thirty years, he'd managed to avoid it. But then came Desiree. She would be the one woman to alter the course of his life, forever.

"Marry me. I can protect you from him."

"What?" Desiree looked at Robert as if he was insane.

"I'm serious. I love you. I'll make you happy. I know I can," Robert said.

"You don't even have a ring!" Desiree tilted her head, a lip curled up.

"Is that the kind of woman you are? You care more about the ring than about the man?" Robert challenged.

"Most people would believe I'm that kind of woman," she said.

"But I have seen a side of you that proves most people wrong, haven't I?"

"Well, the least you could do is get on a knee for me," Desiree pouted.

"That's too cliché. And boring. You wouldn't really like that," Robert said.

Desiree laughed. "Oh, really. I wouldn't. And you think you know what I like, do you? After only knowing me a few weeks?"

"I know you better than you know yourself, I think."

"Is that right?" Desiree studied Robert's eyes. He gazed into hers, unmoving.

Robert picked her up and started to carry her out to his motorcycle. "Let's waste no time, then. We can come back for your things later."

"Wait. I didn't say yes! And even if I did, I couldn't get married looking like this. My face!" Desiree said. "The Justice would think you were the one who hit me. And I really would like to wear something more attractive for my wedding."

"You look stunning. Always. Even with a beat-up face, and wearing pajama pants and a sweatshirt. Even wearing an ass on your head."

Desiree beat his chest. "Robert! Please! Put me down."

Robert sighed and set her down. "Alright. Knock yourself out. It won't make a difference what you wear, I'll be thinking the entire time of taking you home and taking everything off of you anyway."

"Hmph. If you want me to marry you, I have one more stipulation," Desiree said.

"Yes?" Lord Robert smiled.

"I must have Spencer."

"Spencer? What's that? A dog or something?"

"Spencer is a man. My dearest, oldest friend."

Robert narrowed his eyes. "How old?"

Desiree continued. "I always dreamt he would play piano at my wedding. My stipulation is this: if we can get Spencer to play my favorite song today, I'll marry you."

Lord Robert sighed. "Very well. Call him."

Desiree called Spencer, and put her phone on speaker so Robert could hear. "My darling, Spencer! Where are you?"

"Desi? Hey! I'm in Upland. At home."

"No! I can't believe it. I thought you were supposed to be in Zone B, doing a show in The Capital Region."

Lord Robert raised an eyebrow. Did Desiree hope Spencer would be unavailable? Didn't she want to marry him?

"Nope. Gig got cancelled," Spencer said. "New people taking over government didn't like the show. It was too patriotic for them."

"Ah. Strange. So, you wouldn't happen to be available today would you?" Desiree asked.

"Got nothing going on, Desi. Why? Want to hang?"

"Actually, I was wondering if you might be able to play piano at a wedding today?" She looked at Robert and widened her eyes, as if the thought was crazy.

"Say, what?" Spencer asked. "Who's getting married?"

"Well, I am, actually. And I always wanted you to play *Bellais Minuet in D* at my wedding, Spence. Can you?"

"Wait! You and that Lord August guy? Desi," Spencer said. "Are you sure you want to be stuck with him for the rest of your life?"

"No, it isn't him. It's... someone else."

"What?! Why am I just hearing about this?" Spencer asked.

"Oh, it's sort of a last-minute thing... "

"Ah, Desi. Please tell me this new guy's an upgrade from that Lord August fellow."

A half smile crossed Desiree's face as she appraised Lord Robert. "Mmm, I think you might approve of this one."

"I hope you know what you're doing, Desi," Spencer said slowly. "Alright. You know I can't say no to you, kid. Where is the wedding?"

Robert interrupted, "Justice of the Peace. And if you arrive in twenty minutes, I'll pay you ten thousand pins." The other end of the phone was silent.

"Spencer?" Desiree asked him. "Are you still there?"

"Was that your... fiancé?" Spencer asked in a squeaky voice. "Did I just hear him right?"

"Yes," Desiree said, proudly.

"Ten *thousand* pins?"

"You heard me correctly," Lord Robert said, laughing.

"I'll be there... most definitely."

"Good. Then you will get to meet my fiancé. Soon to be husband. Lord Robert Ranfurly," Desiree said.

"Lord Robert Ranfurly? Well, well! Congratulations, Desi! And Lord Ranfurly. Wow." Spencer said, unable to contain his excitement.

After they'd hung up, Robert asked Desiree, "So? Does this mean you are saying yes?"

Desiree looked at him, and took a deep breath. "Very well, then. I'll marry you. Without a ring. And without you getting on a knee. But I will be wearing that forest green di Bianco dress. I don't own anything white, ever since you destroyed the only white dress in my wardrobe."

"Green is my favorite color, my love," Robert said.

They officiated the wedding and she moved into Upland House that day. After that, Robert didn't give August the opportunity to harm her again.

SIX WEEKS AFTER THE WEDDING

"Why do you have to be gone all day? I want to come home to my wife every night, not to an empty house." It was morning, and Robert held Desiree tightly, not wanting to let her get out of bed.

"Robert, I'm the leading role in a film. You don't understand what I do, the hours it takes to train and pour myself into a role. I mean, be grateful at least this film is local. Most of the time I'm filming on location somewhere else across the globe."

"Has August tried to contact you again?"

"If he did, good luck to him getting past your bodyguards."

"Good." Robert nodded. Desiree scowled. "What? You're not still bitter about me having them watch after you, are you?"

"I hate it," she said.

"Well, I hate your work schedule. Maybe there is a way we can work it out to see each other more."

"I have to be on set at four o'clock a.m. for makeup and hair. Then I have to be ready by six for filming. In between the scenes, I'm training with my choreographer. With several fight scenes in this film, the choreography is intense."

"That's insane. How does an actor ever find time for family?" Robert asked.

Desiree laughed. "They don't. Why do you think marriages fall apart so quickly in my world?"

"Well, that is simply unacceptable. We can't let that happen to us, my love." Robert kissed his wife and tried to entice her to stay with him longer. But she pushed him off of her.

"No. I can't be late, Robert. I have to go."

"Where are you headed today? I thought you weren't filming until Monday."

"Today is choreography. I did tell you already. You just forgot. I have to train with Simon," she said, pronouncing the name See-mow, the way people from La Belle Terre said it. She pulled off her nightgown and slipped on yoga pants.

Frustrated, Robert watched his wife leave. He had trouble thinking straight when she wasn't with him. There had to be a way he could get her to stay home more.

That night, Desiree came home at eight o'clock p.m.

"Desiree, training for eight hours? Really? That's insane," Robert said.

"You're telling me? I'm the one who has to do it!" Desiree said. "And I'm famished. A juicy steak sounds divine right about now."

"Alright, let's go out. And listen. I have been thinking all day about a solution to our problem. And I came up with an idea."

"You are full of ideas, Robert," Desiree rolled her eyes. "Meanwhile my hanger increases".

"I'm taking you to Sizzles. You told me they have your favorite steaks. And true, I *am* full of ideas because I'm a genius. You might actually like this one."

"Hmph. Tell me *after* you feed me," she said.

After she'd inhaled her steak and was in happier spirits, he sprung his idea on her. "Why don't we have your choreographer, Simon, is it? Have him move into the house. He can stay in one of the spare bedrooms. You always tell me those rooms are just collecting dust."

"Hmm. That *is* an interesting idea," Desiree said.

"And the room where I practice fencing and martial arts already has mirrors, bars, a professionally installed dance floor. Perfect for your rehearsals," Robert added.

Desiree tilted her head. "Really? Let me run it past Simon."

She did, and the plan seemed to go over well with everyone. A few days later, Simon moved into Upland House. Robert finally got to meet the choreographer his wife had been spending so much time with, and he was a bit alarmed when he saw how good-looking the man was,

"I can't thank you enough for coming up with this idea and allowing me to stay here, Monsieur." Simon's cat-like verdant eyes widened dramatically. He had black, short, and a dark, olive complexion, as most people did who came from the south region of La Belle Terre. He was about six feet tall, and had a trim, muscular frame. Definitely looked like someone who belonged in films.

Robert wondered if he should be jealous of the man. Simon went on, "Desiree said this was a rent-free arrangement? Unbelievable! I was paying an idiotic amount for the tiny apartment on Buckland Street I rented."

"Happy this works well for us all, then. Just as long as you don't keep my wife away from me too much," Robert said, firmly. A clear warning.

As the days passed, Robert's jealousy dissipated. Desiree was at Robert's side during every free minute she could spare, eager to please him in every way, while she usually dreaded having to spend time with Simon, her trainer.

"Simon's so brutal!" she would often say after a hard day of training.

One night when Desiree and Robert were snuggling in bed, she said. "Robert! This was a perfect solution! I love being home and working on choreography here. You *are* a genius." She kissed him passionately.

"You know I'd go to the ends of the earth and back for you, Desi," he whispered.

"You're amazing, my love. The perfect man." Another passionate kiss. "Would you be willing to grant me a little wish?" she whispered.

"Anything. Name it," he said, aching to taste more of her.

"My friend from La Belle Terre, Sophie, is an actress, and I helped her get a part in my film. But now she needs a place to live. Would you be willing to let her stay here, in one of your other dusty, empty rooms?"

"Does she have any terrible living habits I should know about?" he asked.

"She is a perfect saint, darling. Quiet as a mouse. A health nut, doesn't smoke, or have bad digestive issues accompanied by flatulence. I'm sure you'll adore her." Desiree smirked.

Lord Robert chuckled. "Of course, my love...*Any friend of yours is a friend of mine.*"

7

COURTNEY

FLASHBACK – AGE SIXTEEN
Mill Pond

After that day we met in music class, Keith became my new friend. My only real friend to hang out with at school. The football team adopted me as their tagalong because I was Keith's friend. After football practice, I gave a couple of them rides home on my motorcycle, and that definitely won them over.

I told Keith all about Meg and how I hoped he would like her if they ever got to meet, and he said, "I'm sure I'll like her. Any friend of yours is a friend of mine." I wanted them to meet, but I only saw her a couple of times a year when we'd go back to visit my cousins in The Goldens. She could never make it up to visit me.

One time, at school during lunch, Keith and I were sitting alone together. One of Keith's buddies came up to us and asked, "So are you two like, dating now?"

I laughed and said, "No, we're just friends."

After that, Keith used to say things like, "Want to go out to the movies with me? As just friends?" I had a secret crush on him, but no way was I going to let him know. I didn't want to mess up our friendship in case he didn't return my feelings.

Later that same school year, Keith asked me, "So, do you have a date for prom yet?"

"No. Do you?"

"Not yet. Want to go together? As just friends?"

"Okay," I said, maintaining my chill composure. Internally, I was doing back flips and cartwheels.

At prom, during a slow dance, Keith unexpectedly kissed me. It was my very first kiss, and it was worth waiting sixteen years for.

"Yes, Meg, my foot popped. Yes, I felt tingly, and warm, and fuzzy... all those things. It was truly magical."

"Wow," said Meg, who was still waiting to be kissed.

After that, we were no longer "just friends." That whole, "I'll never be a cheerleader" plan went out the window when Keith convinced me I should join the cheer squad so we could see each other more. And I was having the best time of my life.

MILL POND HIGH
YEAR FOUR - WINTER

"I can't believe we won the state championship!" Keith picked me up and kissed me. I'd never been more proud to live in Mill Pond, Cascadia as I *was on that day. It was our senior year, Mill Pond High's football team was undefeated, and my boyfriend, Keith Drake, was the star player of the team. On top of that, I was the captain of the cheer squad, and we were undefeated and going to regionals. For about a week, life was as good as it could get.*

A week later, the football team lost big to the team they played. Following that let down, the cheerleading squad bombed at regionals. It was a bit of a rollercoaster ride, feeling on top of the highest mountain one week, then crushed to pieces a week later when we found out we weren't as great as we thought. Not on a regional level. Plus, as seniors, it was our last year to be a part of it all. For about another two weeks, many tears were shed and life sucked.

After the emotional coaster of football and cheer season ended, springtime came at last. Keith was focused on applying to colleges, and I tried out for a musical in a community theater about thirty minutes away from Mill Pond.

"I got the lead role!" I told Keith a week later after call backs.

"What? That's amazing, babe! But I knew you would. You are perfect for that part and can out-sing anyone."

"This means we won't see each other as much, though," I told him. "Remember last spring when I did the musical?"

"Well, we're just going to have to make the most of every minute we have together, then," Keith lowered his voice. "Swing time, right?"

I winked at him. Swing time was our code for "make out time." Last summer, we'd went to a place on Keith's property that we called the Swing. Keith's family had a hundred acres with a homestead on it that they'd inherited from their great grandparents. A river ran through the property, and there was a huge tree with a rope tied to it that we'd use to swing into the river during the summer months. Near the swing was a private little cove hidden from onlookers and we escaped to that spot whenever we wanted to be alone. I hadn't lost my innocence yet, but last summer, we'd come close.

I knew Keith had already lost his virginity to some random girl at a party, then he'd been with J.C. But I never felt right about it when we crossed certain boundaries. Fortunately, Keith never forced me. During the school year, we'd been too busy to go to the swing and make out. It was too muddy and yuck out anyway. But we were headed into spring, and the weather was getting nice again. Keith made it clear by frequent comments that he couldn't wait to take me back there.

The play rehearsals began, and I became extremely involved in that. The guy who was playing my love interest in the play was in college, really good looking, and really into me. I started to have feelings for him, and became torn about whether I should break up with Keith and see what might happen with the college guy in the play, or stay faithful to Keith and ignore the feelings I was having.

I didn't have to worry about what to do for long, though. Keith beat me to the punch.

"Courtney, I've been thinking, since I'm going away to college soon, and since you're so busy with your play, maybe we should take a break."

"Take a break? Well, yea. I guess I was kind of feeling the same way."

"You were?" Keith asked, surprised.

"Yea. I mean, like you said, you're going to be leaving for college in the fall. Maybe a break makes sense, you know?"

"Oh," Keith said. Why did he sound disappointed? It was his idea.

"I mean, that's what you really want, right?" I asked him.

"Yea. I mean, I think so," he said.

A week later, during lunch at school, I was talking to Meg on the phone, because now that Keith and I weren't dating, I had nobody to hang out with. The entire school rallied around Keith, who was Mr. Popular.

"And he's in college," I told Meg, referring to the guy in the play. "Can you believe it? I'm actually kissing a college guy!"

Keith walked by right when I said that. He glared at me and said, "Wow. I didn't realize you were seeing a college guy. I guess it's a good thing it's totally over between us." He stormed off.

Wait, what just happened? His words cut like a knife. I didn't mean for things to go the way they did.

After that, Keith started hanging out with a new girl. Cindy Smith. Like me, she was also from The Goldens, and had just moved up that year. She was a year behind us in school, had long, curly, copper hair, deep brown eyes and chocolate-colored skin. Not a fake tan. Nothing fake about Cindy. She was an exotic beauty. What was worse, she was a volleyball player. The volleyball team wore bikinis when they played, and her body was flawless. Perfect and proportional. I envied everything about her. Especially her dark, flawless skin, because mine was extremely flawed, and seemed to deflect sunlight.

Keith took Cindy to prom. They were crowned king and queen. Now that he was dating Cindy, all the guys envied Keith, looked up to him as if he was some sort of superhero since he'd landed the most gorgeous girl in school.

After that, high school became Hell School for me. I gave Keith the cold shoulder and tried to focus on my co-star in the play, but all of a sudden all I could see were the college guy's many flaws. His teeth were too crooked, he spit when he said his lines, he had bad breath. The list went on.

I hated Keith. I ached for him. Many, many tears were shed. And as for Cindy Smith. Grr.

I walked past Cindy one day at school, and she was wearing Keith's letterman jacket. An overwhelming urge to punch her face and maim her disgustingly gorgeous smile came over me. I resisted. No doubt, she would have punched me back. Killed me in a fight. She was in way better shape than I was.

MILL POND HIGH
YEAR FOUR - SPRING

My lesson time was now right after Keith's, so I had to cross paths with him once a week outside of school. Keith brought Cindy along to his lessons with him, probably just to irk me. I'd hear her in the room, laughing, singing along (off-key) to the songs he played. Grr.

But Mr. Lyons. That man was no fool. He knew we broke up, so without mentioning it to either of us, he arranged for Keith to be my accompanist at the Spring recital again that year.

"What are you doing here? It's my lesson time," I snapped at Keith when I went into the small music studio for my weekly lesson, and he was sitting on the piano bench.

He huffed. "I guess Mr. Lyons has me being your background musician again. Get over it, because we aren't going to drag Mr. Lyons into our drama and tell him we won't work together just because we broke up."

"I am over it," I snapped back at him.

We practiced once a week for the next three weeks, without saying a word to each other. On the fourth week, at our final practice before recital, Keith stopped playing in the middle of the song.

"I can't do this anymore," he said.

"What? You want me to get another accompanist? Now? The performance is this weekend!" I said, frustrated and angry.

"No, not this. Of course, I'm not going to bail on the performance. I'm talking about us."

I stared at him. "Us? There is no us. Last I checked you had a new girlfriend."

"And you had a new boyfriend," he said.

"I don't have a new boyfriend," I said, looking at him like he was off his granny's rocker.

"You're not kissing College Guy from your play?" he asked me, clearly annoyed.

"I never kissed College Guy for real. We just kissed in the play. He was my love interest in the play." I crossed my arms.

"Oh." Keith shifted on the piano bench. "Well, it has been really sucky. Us not talking. I hate this. I can't see you and not miss you like crazy."

"Really?" I looked into his grey-blue eyes, and saw sadness. The ice between us was melting.

He nodded. "That's why I decided to break up with Cindy."

"What? Why? Wasn't she perfect enough for you?"

"No, she wasn't at all perfect for me," he said.

"Really," I rolled my eyes. "Shooting for higher, huh?"

"She wasn't perfect for me because... the truth is, she wasn't you."

I looked at him, tears threatening to spill from my eyes. "What?" I whispered.

"Not even close," he whispered. "So... you're not planning on dating the play guy?"

"Uh no. I don't like him at all. Not for me. Nope." I shook my head. "He wasn't you," I whispered, a tear trickled down my cheek.

Keith pulled me down to the piano bench next to him, and kissed me. After that, we were inseparable.

Knowing what I know now, I should have thought twice about going to The Swing with Keith. After the separation and all that pent up anger and frustration, we were burning hotter than a blazing wildfire. On our next visit to The Swing, I threw caution to the wind and lost my virginity to Keith Drake.

A month later, I missed my period.

8

LORD ROBERT

PRESENT
Upland House

Sophie first arrived at Upland House while Robert had been at work, and when he came home that night, he saw Sophie and wondered if her and Simon might be related.

Like Simon, Sophie was lean, built like a ballerina, had an olive complexion, and black hair. Her eyes weren't shaped like a cat's, as Simon's were, but were more like a deer's, large and round, the shade of deep, mocha brown. Her hair was cut into a tidy and perfectly smooth bob, a style that complimented her heart-shaped face. Everything about Sophie was tidy and pristine.

She and Simon were speaking in their native language.

"Mais pourquoi?" *But why?* Simon was asking her.

"Elle m'a invité." *She invited me.* Sophie replied.

"Hmph." Simon said, looking a bit annoyed, Robert thought. He wondered why Simon would be annoyed as he walked in on them and interrupted their conversation.

"Yes, Desiree has invited her, and so have I," he said to Simon. Then he turned to greet Sophie. "I'm Lord Robert. You must be Sophie. Desiree speaks very highly of you," Robert held out a hand.

"Oui. Enchanté. I mean, yes. I'm sorry, I'm used to my own language," Sophie said.

"It's fine. I speak Bellais as well. In fact, my mother was from La Belle Terre."

"Ah, bien. What part?"

"The south," he said, remembering his mother's beautiful olive skin. "Is that the part you are from as well?"

"Oui. I'm from a coastal town. Known for our beautiful beaches."

"Isn't that the part you're from, as well, Simon? Do you two already know each other?" Robert asked Simon.

"Oui, we've been acquainted for a few years. I was the fight chore-ographer for a couple of films she was in," Simon explained.

"Thank you so much for allowing me to stay here, Monsieur," Sophie said to Robert.

"You are more than welcome. How is your room? Is there anything you need?"

"The room is perfect, merci. No, I don't need anything more."

Desiree walked in and squealed. "Sophie!" She ran to her friend and kissed her on each cheek. "My dear Sophie. You've met my most delectable husband, I see. Now remember, he is *all* mine. You don't get to share him."

At times, Desiree acted in ways Robert neither understood nor particularly liked. Perhaps she was joking, but he didn't really find joking about their relationship amusing.

"Simon, you must show Sophie around. Whenever we aren't working, your job is to be an amazing host to her. You must make her feel like she is at home here."

Robert noticed the way Sophie appraised Simon, and thought she seemed pleased at the arrangement. But he didn't sense that the feelings were mutual on Simon's side.

That's why, when two days later Robert came home early from work, he was surprised when he knocked on Simon's bedroom door. He wanted to ask him if he'd be willing to work some extra hours as his private trainer. Simon called out, "Come in," so Robert opened the door, only to find Simon with Sophie, undressed and intwined with bed sheets barely covering them.

"Excuse me. I'm sorry, I..." Lord Robert stammered.

"No apology needed, Monsieur. We are all adults here. Did you want something?" Simon asked, nonchalant.

"Yes. Well, I um..." Robert avoided looking at the couple as he went on. "I was wondering if you wanted to earn some more money by being my private trainer. I'd like to take my fencing to the next level."

Simon raised his eyebrows. "Hmm. I'm busy playing host to this little minx, but not getting paid for that." Sophie smacked him across his face. Simon laughed. "See? She is far more fun than she comes across. Oui. I will be happy to train you, Lord Robert."

Robert left them, feeling awkward. He knew people from La Belle Terre were far more outwardly sensual than people from The Greens. It was a different culture than he was accustomed to. Desiree had spent lots of time in La Belle Terre, which is part of the reason her behavior sometimes shocked him, made him uncomfortable. But she was wild, impossible to tame, and he knew it wasn't right to force her to be different on his account. Still, would he ever get used to that part of her?

The next day, Robert was passing by the parlor where Desiree and Simon usually rehearsed choreography when he overheard Desiree and Sophie in an argument.

"Does it really shock you that Simon would want me? What, do you think I'm not good enough for him? Or could it be that you're just jealous?" Sophie asked.

"Jealous?" Desiree laughed. "Please. I'm married to perfection. I'm certainly not jealous of you and Simon."

Robert smiled to himself and kept walking. He didn't hear the rest of the conversation that passed between the women.

"I just don't want you to get hurt," Desiree continued. "We both know what a player Simon is. I'd like to see you with someone who will be faithful, Sophie."

"Desiree, do you think I'm a fool?" Sophie asked, a hand on her hip.

"What? Of course not! Why would you ask me that?"

"You are always the actress. Even with me, your friend who has known you since before you were ever on stage," Sophie said.

"What is it you are getting at, Sophie?"

"I've seen you with him. With Simon." Sophie stared into Desiree's eyes, trying to read her. Desiree's blue eyes could have been stone, they remained so unreadable. Sophie continued. "When Robert was at work. I came home early one day and walked in on you and Simon in his bedroom."

Desiree looked Sophie in the eyes, and gently said, "And? What is it you think you saw, exactly, Sophie?"

"I don't think. I know. Neither of you had a stitch of clothing on, and you were fully engaged in making love. Deny it all you want, but I saw with my own eyes."

Desiree laughed. "What you saw was Simon showing me how to fake the love scene in my latest film, Sophie. We were wearing special coverings, which made it look as if we were completely naked. But we weren't. There is nothing, absolutely no feelings between Simon and me. But I wouldn't feel comfortable doing that scene with my co-star had he not shown me a way to pull it off. My co-star repulses me."

"Really? You were wearing coverings? It looked so real," Sophie said.

"Well, that was the idea, wasn't it?"

Sophie laughed, relieved. "Yes, I suppose so. I've actually had to film scenes like that too. And I've worn those special coverings. Yes. I see now. So, you really don't have feelings for him, then?"

"Heavens no, Sophie! Have you taken a look at the man I'm married to? I'm madly in love with Lord Robert! But please, please don't tell Robert about those rehearsals between Simon and me. I know he won't understand. He isn't an actor, isn't from our world."

"Oui. I understand. I'll keep it between us," Sophie said, nodding.

"Thank you. No doubt, we'd all be thrown out into the street if he found out," Desiree said.

"Ah, that would be horrific. I appreciate that you arranged for me to live here, and for getting me the role in your film. I promise your secret is safe with me," Sophie said. "But Desiree, what if Simon is in love with you?"

"That's ridiculous. Simon and I are nothing but friends. There's never been feelings between us, I'm sure of it."

"I hope you're right. Because I have been in love with Simon a very long time. And this is the first time he's ever paid attention to me. He was always with you before when we all lived in La Belle Terre."

"Sophie, you're perfect for him. Exactly what he needs. He'd be an idiot to not be in love with you."

A moment later, Simon came into the room, wrapped his arms around Sophie and kissed her neck.

"Simon," Desiree wagged a finger at him. "You're an hour late!" Desiree said. "We have to begin rehearsal. Would you like to stay and watch, Sophie?" Desiree asked. "Maybe Simon can show you how to do our latest move. You'll catch on quick, you're incredibly flexible."

"Yes, the perfect ballerina," Simon said.

"I'd love to," Sophie said.

TWO WEEKS LATER

Lord Robert had to lecture at a university in The Capital City, and as usual stayed with Peter and Nina.

"You got married! And didn't even care to tell us?" Nina wasn't happy.

"It was sudden," Robert said.

"Marriage isn't something people should rush into, Robert," Peter said.

"I don't remember asking for your opinion," Robert snapped.

"What's gotten into you? You're not usually like this," Peter said.

"I just don't think it's anyone's place to tell me who I should marry, and you both seem bent on butting into my affairs. It isn't your business."

"Woah. Sounds like that woman has already changed you!" Nina said, offended. "You know, the right person should bring out the best in you. But I don't like this side of you we're seeing."

"You've never even met my wife, and you're insinuating she isn't the right person for me?" Robert was furious. He left The Capital City a day earlier than planned, at odds with Peter and Nina.

Once back in Upland, as he drove down his driveway to Upland House, Lord August Wellington's sports car was leaving. "What was he doing here?" Robert wondered. Heat boiled and rose inside him.

Instead of driving into the garage, he parked in the circle driveway and stormed into the house, in search of Desiree.

"Looking for your wife, Lord Robert?" Simon asked him.

"Oh, Simon. I didn't hear you behind me. Yes, have you seen her?"

"She went out about the same time Lord August left. Perhaps they went somewhere together?"

Robert clenched his jaw and shook his head. "Why would she do that? Besides, I saw Lord August drive off alone."

"Oh, well. You know your wife. She is probably out for a walk or something," Simon said.

"Simon, do you know why Lord August was here? He didn't threaten Desiree, did he?"

"I don't know, Monsieur." Simon continued, "I'm not sure what they spoke about. But it must have been important, they spoke for a good hour."

Lord Robert blew out air and tried to cool his head. He needed to calm down, or the rage he felt would consume him. "An hour? What did they need to discuss? And why for an hour, Simon?"

It seemed to Robert as if Simon was being careful to choose words. "Em... je ne sais pas." *I don't know.*

"Did you overhear anything they said?"

"Not really. We were rehearsing choreography for our film when he was announced. Desiree excused herself and went to the foyer to speak with him." Simon paused but seemed to be holding something back.

"Surely you could hear them in the foyer. It is right next to where you rehearse," Lord Robert said through gritted teeth.

"Well, I'm afraid they didn't exactly *stay* in the foyer." Simon laughed uncomfortably and shifted from one leg to the other.

"Where did they go, if they didn't stay in the foyer?" Robert asked, his abdomen in knots.

"Desiree invited Lord August into your study, then closed the doors." Simon said quickly, then bit his lip.

For a moment, Lord Robert saw nothing but red. Then he gave Simon a glaring look before he stormed into his study and scanned the room. The couch in the study looked the same as it always looked, it didn't appear that anyone had been lying on it. Nothing seemed out of place.

What were they doing in my study with the doors closed? For an hour? "If Desiree and August were having..." Lord Robert started to say out loud but stopped himself. He didn't want to speak something into existence. Besides, it wasn't logical. How could Desiree still want to be with August? He was awful to her, and Robert treated her like royalty, gave her everything.

Robert couldn't see or think clearly. The only thought he had in his mind was that he'd like to kill Lord August. He went to his desk, and opened the hidden drawer where he kept his gun.

✦━◆━➤ 9 ◄━◆━✦

LORD ROBERT

PRESENT
Upland House

"Good to know this is where it should be," Lord Robert said. He pulled his gun out and put it in his jacket pocket.

Lord Robert was finished putting up with August. This time the man had come into his home, into his study. When it came to Desiree, he would go to any lengths to protect her. He stormed out of the house in a rage and headed to his car, with every intention to find August and deal with him.

Desiree was walking through the rose garden when she saw him heading toward his car. "Robert! You're home early, my love!" She ran up to him and threw her arms around his neck. He stiffened. By the flushed look upon her face, Robert guessed she'd been on a walk.

"Why are you acting like the Great Stone Wall of Upland? Is that any way to greet me after not seeing me for a week?" She played with a stray curl that fell out of his man bun. "You didn't fall in love with another woman over in The Capital, did you?"

"If I had, would it really matter to you? I mean, what with you spending so much time with August Wellington and all. Perhaps you regret marrying me, and would rather run back to his arms?"

Desiree laughed and looked at Lord Robert as if he was out of his mind. "What are you talking about? Don't be ridiculous!"

"Am I being ridiculous? I just saw him drive away from the house, and Simon said you were with him for a good hour in my study. What did you two find to do in my study that took an hour, I wonder?"

Desiree laughed again. "Robert! It sounds like you're insinuating that I made love to August."

Robert tried to maintain his composure, but by the way he clenched his jaw and tightened his right hand into a fist, his icy fury was evident. "You were in there for a good hour with the doors closed. What exactly *were* you in there doing with him?"

"Robert, please. You are angry with me before you've even allowed me to explain."

Desiree was not wrong, Lord Robert admitted to himself. He was far beyond angry. He was actually contemplating murder. Lord Robert tried to slow his heart rate. To see clearly. To calm down. "Fine. Explain away, Desiree."

She put her hand on his chest, initially causing him to stiffen, to protect himself. But she persisted to win him over as she gently kneaded her fingers in, and after a moment, the heat of her touch did what she aimed for, sent him under her spell. She spoke in her low, husky voice, and once again he found himself unable to break away from watching her plump, pink lips as she spoke. He *wanted* her to convince him of her innocence.

"Lord August came to speak with *you,* actually,"she said. "Not me. He told me it was about your brother." She studied his face, watched his eyes move from her lips to meet her gaze.

"My brother?"

"Yes. Robert, I didn't even know you had a brother. Were you planning on sharing that with me sometime?" Desiree raised an eyebrow.

Lord Robert looked at her, confused. "I- well, I... it never even crossed my mind. My brother is of no consequence, Desiree. He's a waste of a life. How does Wellington have anything to do with him?"

"He said your brother lost to him in gambling. Apparently, he can't pay his debts and he owes August forty thousand pins! Now August is saying that you have to pay him, since your brother can't."

Lord Robert scoffed. "So that is Lord August's excuse to come here, is it? No doubt he wanted to see you. To be alone with you. So, Desiree. It took you two minutes to tell me that. And yet it took August an entire hour to tell you the same thing?"

"No, my dear. What took an hour was that I tried to convince him that you shouldn't have to pay, of course."

"You tried to convince him? How did you try to convince him, Desiree?"

"Please, you are terrible. The way you're looking at me. Do you think that I slept with him to convince him?" Desiree removed her hand and broke away from him. "Honestly. I don't like this green monster side of you, Robert. It's sad because I actually had some *good news* to tell you. But now, I regret it. I regret marrying a man like you, who believes the absolute worst about me."

She ran into the house, slamming the front door behind her. Robert stared after her for a few seconds, then ran after her. She'd already gone upstairs to their master bedroom and locked the doors by the time he was back in the house.

Robert ran up the stairs and banged on the bedroom doors. "Let me in, Desiree."

"No, go away! I hate you."

"Look, I'm sorry. I was angry. I was wrong to think those things. Please," Robert's tone softened. "Please let me in."

"No! I'll never forgive you for thinking so terribly of me."

"I said I was sorry. I missed you while I was away, and I even brought something back to give you. Please open the door, my love." Lord Robert said tenderly.

"What did you bring me?" She asked.

"I'll show you if you open the doors," he coaxed.

Desiree opened one of the doors a crack, and said, "I want you to be happy when I tell you this news. It means everything to me."

"Tell me what news, my love?" Robert said, his face as close to hers as he could get through the crack of the door. "May I come in?"

Desiree slowly opened the door, and he slipped into the room, softly closing the door behind him and locking it. He pulled his wife against him, and bit into her neck.

"Mmm. I missed you," he whispered, and he felt her melt into his arms. "I hated being away from you. It was torture." He picked her up and carried her toward the bed.

"Robert, I have news I need to tell you. Remember?"

"What news, my love," he said, still enjoying the taste of her neck.

"You might want to be sitting down," she said. Robert sat on the bed, still fully engaged in wanting to devour his wife. Desiree was now on his lap.

"Wait here," she whispered. "I've got a little surprise for you," she giggled, and got up, then crossed over to her dresser.

When she opened her lingerie drawer, a half-smile crossed Lord Robert's face, "I think I'm going to like this surprise..." He threw his coat off and started to unbutton his shirt.

"I hope so," Desiree laughed, and tilted her head sideways. She pulled something out and hid it behind her back.

"What do you have? A little new treat to model for me?" Lord Robert asked, a glorious smile crossed his face.

"No, my love." She held up the hand that was behind her back and dangled something, tiny and yellow.

"Is that something you wear?" he curled up a lip and raised an eyebrow.

Desiree giggled. "No,"

"Oh. No? Is it something I wear?"

She snorted. "No! You ninny. These are booties." Lord Robert still looked baffled. "Booties. For a baby! I'm pregnant!"

Time seemed to freeze in midair. That was the last thing he was expecting to hear.

✦→ 10 ←✦

COURTNEY

MILL POND HIGH
YEAR FOUR · SPRING
Mill Pond, Cascadia

I held my breath as I waited for the result of the home pregnancy test. Then, to my surprise and horror, I saw the little plus sign, bold and blue.

I didn't see any other choice except to abort.

I never saw myself becoming a mother. It wasn't even a thought in my head. I'd never been the type of girl to play dolls, or house. Never liked to babysit. Seventeen-year-old Courtney thought babies were loud, annoying, and smelled like poop most of the time.

Sure, maybe one day, in the far away future, maybe then. Maybe by the time I was thirty I'd want kids. But before then, I had dreams. Big dreams.

No way was I going to tell anyone about the mistake. First off, both Keith's parents and mine would be furious. They were super big on waiting to have sex until marriage, and to admit the truth meant eternal damnation in their eyes.

No. I believed I had to keep the secret to myself. I had no real friends in which to confide in Mill Pond, except Keith. I'd kept in touch with Meg, but I was afraid to tell her. Ever since she'd gone to a church camp, she'd become extremely religious.

As much as I wanted to tell Keith, I was afraid. He had big dreams of his own, and this would mess everything up for him.

I could see only one possible solution and that was to abort. I made an appointment and went alone to the doctor. It was terrifying. While I was in the waiting room for the appointment, the nurse came out and spoke with me.

"I'm so sorry, Ms. Lane, but the doctor has an emergency in his family. His wife's in labor with their first child. He'll have to reschedule your appointment for another time."

A few days later, the doctor called me.

"Hello, Ms. Lane. This is Dr. Martin. I'm very sorry I was unable to do the procedure the day you came in for your appointment. As the nurse explained, my wife was in labor, and I didn't want to risk missing the birth of my first child."

"I understand. But the issue now is that I'm already six weeks pregnant. I would like to have the procedure done soon. Can we reschedule my appointment in the next couple of days?"

"Actually, Ms. Lane, I know this is going to be difficult for you, but I've had a change of heart about performing abortions since the birth of my child. It has been weighing on my conscience for quite some time now, and I've finally made my decision to stop the practice of doing abortions. I'm afraid you will have to find another doctor."

I was stunned. I called three other doctors and tried to get in that week. But not one of them could fit me in. Not for another three weeks. At that point, I'd be almost ten weeks into the pregnancy.

I didn't know who to talk to. In desperation, I decided to call Meg.

"Hey Meg! How are you?" I said over the phone.

"Crow? Oh wow! I haven't heard from you since last winter. I thought you were mad at me!" Meg said.

"Mad at you? Why did you think that?" I asked her, knowing full well why she thought that. She had been on a high horse about how she'd changed because of some camp she went to that told her she needed to read the Scriptures.

I felt like that camp had stolen my best friend and replaced her with a scary clone. I hung up on her that day, hurt and angry. After that, I couldn't bring myself to call her again.

"Come on, Crow. We both know how bad it ended the last time we spoke. You hung up on me."

"I guess I did," I said, afraid the conversation might be headed right back to where we'd left it.

"You had a right to hang up on me. I was being a jerk."

"What? Well-uh..."

"I'm sorry, Crow. For how I was acting that day. I really am."

I sighed. "I'm sorry too, for getting so mad and hanging up on you. But you did practically crush my skull in with all the scriptures you cracked over my head. I understand that you found religion, but I'm just not into all that, Meg."

"I know. It was just that I was super excited about my new faith. It was all new to me then. But boy, I really wish I could have a do over of that phone conversation. I hope you'll forgive me."

"It's okay, Meg. I do," I told her.

"I've missed you, Courtney."

"I've missed you, too, Meg."

"I actually have something to tell you..." Meg started to say, then broke off. I knew her well, and by the sound of her voice, something was wrong.

"What is it?"

"I was on that spiritual high horse for a couple months, Crow. I made a few enemies, the way I acted. Started to look down on people, didn't see I was being prideful, actually behaving the opposite of what the Scriptures teach. Then I was reading this part in the Scriptures that said God brings down the proud, but lifts up the humble. Boy, was that a warning to me."

"A warning? What do you mean?"

"Well, I got a major crush on a guy at school. He wasn't exactly a good boy, if you know what I mean."

"Yea?"

"All of a sudden I was obsessed with him. I just wanted to find a way to get his attention. One night, I went to a party because I heard he'd be there. Sure enough, he was. Partying. Drinking and doing weed. He started to pay attention to me, and offered me a joint. I wanted to impress him so much that I gave in, and partied with him, made out with him. I drove myself home that night and got in a car crash. Almost died, and now I'm in a wheelchair, for God only knows how long."

I was speechless. Silent for a long time. I could hear Meg quietly sniffling on the other end. Finally, I said, "Oh my gosh, Mouse! I feel terrible! I had no idea!"

"Talk about learning the hard way, right?" she said.

I started crying. All the fear and pain of my situation seemed like nothing compared to what Meg had been through. Was going through. And to think I hadn't called her and had no idea all that time. "Mouse, I'm so sorry. That's... I-I should have called."

She was crying audibly now. "I've wanted to call you for so long, Courtney. But I was afraid you hated me."

"I could never hate you! I wish I could fly down and see you, Mouse!"

"I can't even climb up into our tree house anymore. Pretty sad, huh?"

"We could make a pulley, rope you up, and hoist you into the treehouse," I suggested.

Mouse busted up laughing. "Man, I've missed you, Courtney. Are you and that Keith guy still together?" she asked.

I sighed.

"Oh no," Meg said. "You broke up?"

"No. No, we're together. But Meg, talk about messing things up. You know how our parents told us about all the horrible diseases people get when they have sex, and how we swore we would never do it?"

Meg laughed her funny sounding laugh through her nose. "Yep. I remember. Your mom did a great job terrifying us to keep us out of trouble."

I went on, "And remember what my mom used to always say?"

"It only takes one time." We both said it in unison, and she laughed. Then she paused.

"Wait. Are you trying to tell me that you and Keith..." Meg stopped before having to say the rest, but we both knew what she meant.

"Yea... But only once. And now-" I started to say.

Meg jumped in and finished my sentence. "Oh no! You're pregnant!"

"Yea."

"Courtney! How scary! Have you told your parents?"

"No way! And you have to swear... on your new religion, or the Scriptures, or whatever... that you will never, ever tell anyone. Ever."

"Okay, okay. I promise. I won't tell. What does Keith have to say about it?"

"He doesn't know. I wanted to get an abortion before he found out. But now I can't find a doctor, and... Meg, I can feel it. I mean, there is definitely something different going on in there. I just... I don't think I can get rid of it now. I think I could have last week, but now... should I? Would it be wrong?"

99

Meg was really quiet, and I wondered if she was holding back, afraid to say what she really thought. Finally, she asked, "You can feel it? Really? How many months are you?"

"Almost seven weeks."

"And you can feel it. Wow. That's amazing."

"What do I do, Mouse?"

"I don't know. I think you should at least tell Keith. He deserves to know, right? I mean, he's the dad. Shouldn't he get to weigh in on the decision?"

"Keith doesn't deserve this. He has plans to go to college. He has dreams. I don't want to ruin his life. That doesn't seem like the right thing to do, does it? I really love him, Mouse."

"I wish I could meet this guy who stole my BFF's heart," she said sadly.

"Are you mad at me, Meg?"

"Never!"

"Disappointed?"

"No! No way!" Meg paused. "Courtney..."

"Yea?"

"I've learned a lot about my faith after my accident, and... it isn't like I don't still mess up a lot. But I'm learning that God's love is huge. Powerful. Bigger than my mistakes. Somehow, knowing I'm loved like that, it gives me strength to get through every day."

"Wow. I'm glad your faith is helping you, Meg."

"Thanks. But I'm telling you this because I want you to know you are loved too. God loves you, Courtney. He's bigger than our mistakes. And He works in mysterious ways. I mean, what if... what if God already knew you and Keith were going to be together that one time, and He planned for you to have a baby? Think about all the people who try for years and never get pregnant. But you were with Keith one time and did get pregnant. Maybe that baby isn't a mistake, but is part of a bigger plan."

I laughed. "I don't know about that," I said.

"Well, whatever you decide, I love you, Courtney," Meg continued. "I'll always have your back. You're my bestie."

"Ahh," I said, unable to stop my nose from itching and the tears from welling up. "Stop that! Now look what you made me do." We both laughed and cried our eyes out for a long time that day.

Over the next couple of weeks, Meg called me every day. Those phone conversations we had were like warm cups of tea on blistery, stormy days.

I could feel the baby growing, and my conscience started to scream at me that it would be wrong to end its life. I had no idea what I was going to do with a baby, or when I was going to finally admit I was pregnant to people. I still hadn't told anyone, and other than occasional bouts of morning sickness, I wasn't showing any outward signs that I was expecting.

My dreams of becoming a famous actress started to morph into different dreams. I started imagining what the baby was going to look like. In my imaginings, sometimes the baby would be a girl, sometimes a boy. Over the weeks that passed, mysteriously, almost as if some invisible power was at work, everything in me was being changed. What I wanted in life was changing, and I had no control over it. That beating heart and tiny life inside me was strong enough to overpower me, my desires, my tastebuds, my sleep schedule.

TWO WEEKS LATER

Keith got a job and was working at a restaurant in the town thirty minutes away, so we didn't see each other outside of school much that spring. We hadn't returned to The Swing since the night he got me pregnant. Then Graduation Day arrived, and our senior class went to a theme park that night.

I was feeling a little too queasy to ride a rollercoaster, not to mention there were all the warning signs not to ride if pregnant. So, I walked around *the park with Keith and a few of the football players and watched them while they went on the rides. I felt like an old lady.*

"Courtney, what's wrong? You usually love roller coasters. Are you sick?" Keith asked me.

"Yea, not feeling too good. But I didn't want to miss Grad Night."

"Okay, well, can you at least ride the tram with me? There's amazing views from up there," Keith said. "And we haven't been alone together for what feels like forever."

"I guess I could try riding a tram," I said, dreading what might happen if I did, but wanting to be alone with Keith again.

On the tram, Keith said. "Courtney, there's something I want to ask you."

"What's up?" I asked, wondering why he looked so perplexed. "Something wrong?"

"No. It's just that I got accepted to the college I want to go to. It's about two hours away."

"What? Really? That's- that's amazing! I'm so happy for you, Keith." I really, truly was happy for him. But, at the same time, I was heartbroken. I still had no idea what I was going to do about the baby.

"Courtney, I've missed you so much. It's been too long since we could be alone. Sorry I've been working so much, but I really wanted to save money."

"It's okay. I've missed you too, Keith."

"Look, I know things are changing so fast. But I want you to know that, even though I'll be leaving for college in a couple months, I can't imagine my life without you." He got down on one knee, causing the tram to sway back and forth. I nearly puked but swallowed it back.

"Careful, um. I don't feel good, remember?"

"Oops. Sorry 'bout that." He pulled a little velvet box out of his pocket and opened it. Inside was a beautiful diamond ring. "Courtney, will you marry me?"

I'm pretty sure my mouth hit the tram floor.

"What?"

"I mean, we can wait. Until after college. But I don't want anyone else. Just you. I love you, Courtney."

Tears flowed down my cheeks. "I love you too," I whispered.

Then I realized I had to tell him.

"Keith, I've been wanting to tell you something. It might make you change your mind about wanting to marry me."

Right at that moment, the tram stopped moving. It was common for the tram to stop, due to people tripping as they got on and off, so we didn't panic. But the sudden stop made the car swing more, and I felt that urge to vomit again.

He was still on his knee, holding the ring. "Nothing could make me change my mind. Unless... you didn't cheat on me, did you?"

"No! Never! No, I wouldn't cheat. But I don't want you to give up your dreams for me, Keith."

He laughed. "What? That's crazy, I'm not giving up any dreams. Having you is my dream."

I sucked air in through my teeth. "Maybe not after you hear what I'm about to tell you."

"Oh, come on. Just say what you have to say, Courtney. I'm obviously not going anywhere."

"Yea, you're kind of stuck up here with me, aren't you?" I laughed, nervous about how he was going to react.

"So, what's going on?" he asked.

"Remember that last time we were at The Swing?"

"I'll never forget it, Courtney. I just wish we could do it again."

"Yea. Well, um. I'm pregnant."

Keith dropped the ring.

"Oh no!" I cried out. We both got down on our hands and knees and started searching for it in the bottom of the tram. I noticed there were little *holes in the corners of the tram car that a ring could easily slip through. "Be careful, Keith! Don't move too fast, if this thing tips too much, the ring could slip right out of one of those holes."*

"Have you felt it anywhere in here?" he asked in a panic.

"No!"

We searched until finally he said, "Got it!"

We both sat on the floor of the tram and laughed, relieved.

"Wow, Courtney. Wow."

"That was a close one," I said.

"No kidding." He looked at me. "This little thing here is the reason I've been working like a dog!"

"Oh. Wow. I had no idea that was why..." I trailed off.

"So..." Keith said. "You were saying..." He gulped. "You're definitely sure?"

I nodded. "I've seen a doctor and everything. But my parents don't know. Our parents are going to be furious if they find out, Keith..."

"Yea. You're right about that."

"I'm so sorry. I never meant for this to happen," I said.

"What do you mean, you're sorry? I had a part to play in this too, right?"

I was quiet, not really knowing what to say. Keith slid over on the bottom of the tram to sit next to me. He put an arm around my waist and pulled me in close to him. The movement in the tram made my stomach churn.

"Courtney?" Keith searched my eyes. "What do you want to do?"

Without warning, a tear started trickling down my cheeks. I turned my head away from him and wiped it off. I felt like such an idiot.

"Baby, you know I love you, right? You know this doesn't have to be a bad thing. It isn't like you're some girl I regret being with. I want to be with you forever, anyway."

I half laughed. "Keith, you don't have to say all that. Nobody is asking you to give up your life for me. For this," I pointed to my belly.

He looked at my belly. "Wow. A baby is in there. Our baby. Can I feel it?" He put his hand on my belly.

"Not yet. It is still too small at almost nine weeks, only about the size of a raspberry. But the doctor says it has eyes and a nose, and little hands, legs, and feet are forming. I'm supposed to get an ultrasound at ten weeks."

"Can I come with you?"

"Of course, Keith. I'd love that."

"Baby, my feelings for you are real. But what about you? Do you feel the same way about me? Do you want us to be together?"

I carefully scooted myself up onto the tram bench, and Keith got up to sit next to me. I looked outside the tram, at the beautiful snowcapped mountains that surrounded us.

"I have decided I want this baby," I whispered, then turned to meet his gaze. "I'm scared to death, but I just feel like I can't give it up, you know?"

He smiled. "Okay. But what about me? Do you want me in your life?"

"Of course, Keith. Without a doubt."

"Without a doubt, huh? Like, can you see us together when we're old?"

I laughed. "Honestly? I can't think that far ahead." Keith laughed too.

"Yea, people say that all the time in the movies, but I can't think that far ahead either. I just know I can't imagine life without you in it."

"Same here," I whispered.

"Wait. I have an idea," he said.

"What?" I looked at him. He had a strange look on his face.

"Let's get married now."

I laughed. "Oh. Okay. Like now, now? Up here in the tram?"

He laughed. "No, you moron. Like this summer. Next month. Then come with me to college. Our parents will never have to know I got you pregnant before we got married. What do you say?"

I looked at him, and let the idea soak in.

"Courtney-coo. Come on, I've been saving up for months to buy this ring. Please don't leave me hangin.'"

I laughed. "You mean literally?" I said, standing up and looking over the edge of the tram. I regretted it instantly. I couldn't stop the puke from ejaculating out. I held my head over the edge of the tram until the vomit finished streaming down to hundreds of feet below.

"Oops. Sorry, whoever's down there," I said.

"Now I get it," Keith smacked himself in the head with a palm. "Why you can't ride the rides today. You're not sick."

"You just figured that out, huh?" I laughed.

"Even after that disgusting display, I still love you," he said.

"Okay, Keith. I'm in. I'll marry you!" I said, feeling the joy start to bubble up inside. Then I realized we only had a month to plan a wedding. "Next month!" I squeaked out.

In a manner of minutes, my circumstances unexpectedly turned around, and on a tram ride, no less. We started to kiss, but it was terrible, the taste of throw up in my mouth. I really needed mouthwash.

Grad night. What a memory.

Somehow, I'd really messed up, but just as Meg had reassured me, things were going to turn out okay. All those prayers she was praying must have been doing their job or something.

Meg had been there for me during those scary weeks when I cried over the phone. How I wished I could have cried with her in person. Felt her hugs. How I wished I'd been a better friend to her through her own devastating crisis.

She was supposed to have been my Maiden of Honor at the wedding. But her car accident had done internal damage that her doctor didn't see coming. None of us saw it coming. A week before the wedding, she passed, unexpectedly. Her last words to me were, "Courtney, that baby is a gift. Maybe you think it was unplanned, but God has a plan in mind. Always."

I almost called the wedding off after she died; I was such a wreck. But Keith reminded me that if we waited, my pregnancy would start to show, so we decided to go through with it. Later I was grateful we did.

If only Meg could have been with me on my wedding day, and if only she could have met Keith, and my first-born baby boy, Nicholas, and my daughter, Laurel, who was born a year later.

11

LORD ROBERT

PRESENT
Upland House

With the new distraction of Desiree becoming pregnant, Robert's feelings of hatred for Wellington dissipated.

The filming ended a couple weeks later, and Simon and Sophie moved out of Upland House to go stay in a friend's flat in La Belle Terre. Even with the slightest expansion of her waistline, Desiree was paranoid that she looked fat. Desiree insisted they keep the pregnancy a secret. "You can't let the paparazzi know I'm pregnant. I don't want anyone to know. I don't want people taking pictures of me as a fat cow."

"Desiree, you don't look like a fat cow. Nobody has any idea you are pregnant! The staff doesn't even know yet. And I think you look even more beautiful with my child growing inside your gorgeous belly."

"You lie to me! I do not. I look terrible and nothing fits the same anymore. If you don't keep the paparazzi out of our lives, Robert, I'll divorce you."

"As you wish." Lord Robert said. "But I'm not sure how we'll keep it a secret from them. If the staff finds out, they may very well slip up and tell people."

"Fire the staff! I don't want this secret getting out."

"The only way to keep it from everyone is to get out of The Greens, Desiree."

"Then let's leave. We can go to Zone B or The Tropics."

"Or... have you ever been to Vinosa? I own a villa there that overlooks the ocean. Nobody should recognize you in Vinosa; the people there have their own film stars they follow. They don't pay attention to what is happening in The Greens."

"You have a villa that overlooks the ocean? In Vinosa? And I'm only just now hearing about it? I've always wanted to go to Vinosa. Sounds like a perfect solution, my genius of a husband." The idea won Robert a passionate kiss, which is what he was aiming for.

Vinosa, which was on the main continent, across a channel and several hours drive from Upland, was where they lived for the remaining months of the pregnancy. The paparazzi never discovered where they were, and the pregnancy remained a secret.

After a few months, they learned they were going to have a baby girl. Boots, socks, bibs, onesies, blankets, and stuffies in pinks, purples, and reds filled up the nursery in the house. Robert and Desiree bought everything in Vinosa, which was known to have the finest quality clothing in the world.

The day finally arrived when their bundle of joy would come into the world. Lord Robert stayed with Desiree, stroking her hair through labor. As the doctor at last pulled the baby out he said, "Yep, it is a girl, just as expected."

Feeling unsure, and overwhelmed with all sorts of emotion, Lord Robert held his tiny bundle in his arms. "She's so tiny. I'm not sure I'm holding her right." The nurse in the room showed him how to support the baby's neck. "She has your red hair, my love." Robert was forever changed as he held his newborn daughter in his arms. "What should we name her?"

"Elizabeth," Desiree whispered. "After your mother." Robert had never shared anything about his mother with his wife, but it meant the world to him that Desiree wanted to name their daughter after her.

A few minutes later, the doctor said. "Wait a second. What is this? Keep pushing, Desiree," The doctor ordered. "You're not done. There's another one coming!"

"What? Another one?" Lord Robert didn't understand what was happening. "How can there be another one?"

Desiree pushed, and soon the doctor pulled another red matted head out and cut the second one's umbilical cord.

"Well, well! Looks like you're going to need some tiny blue onesies for this one. It's a boy!" The doctor beamed. He cleaned off the baby and handed the second little bundle to Desiree to hold. The doctor said, "Nice when there are two parents, and its twins. You'll need both sets of arms for these two."

The nurse interrupted. "But now they both need to fill their little bellies."

Robert sat next to Desiree on the bed as the nurse set the babies on each of the mother's breasts. "This is utterly exhausting," Desiree said. "Now I really am a cow."

Once the babies were asleep, Robert and Desiree each took turns holding the infants, trading them back and forth.

"And what will you name the boy?" the nurse asked them.

"Robert? Do you have a favorite name for a boy?" Desiree asked her husband.

"I had a favorite book as a child. It was about a brave boy named Luke. I've always liked that name, Luke," he said.

"And I've always liked the name Lucas," she said. "That's it then, his name is Lucas, and you can call him Luke for short."

The day his twins were born was Robert's happiest memory.

Once the twins were a month old, Lord Robert rented a private jet and flew his little family of four home. Desiree already looked like she had lost all her weight, and both her and Robert were missing the comforts of Upland House. She couldn't wait to decorate the babies' rooms there.

The staff still had no idea about the pregnancy or the birth of the twins, and Robert decided to transfer his butler and maids who were hired for the Upland House to Ranfurly Castle in Knoxfordshire, because he worried they might spill something about the twins to the press. He hired a butler and a maid from Vinosa, as well as a nurse maid, and they all moved into the Upland House. This would eliminate the chance of gossip flying around about the twins, because his Vinosian staff didn't know anyone in Upland.

A few days after they returned to Upland House, Robert went into parliament, and word spread quickly that Lord and Lady Ranfurly had returned, although nobody knew where they'd been. A day after Robert's first day back to parliament, August showed up at Robert's house. It was during Robert's normal work hours, but Robert hadn't gone into work. He was home in his study, and saw Wellington drive up the circle driveway and park his car in front of the house.

"That man is relentless. I'm going to need to buy a security gate," Lord Robert thought. The old fiery rage he'd felt before Desiree became pregnant once again raised up its ugly head.

Robert went outside to meet August. The last thing he wanted was for August to ring the doorbell, wake the babies, and hear their cries. Rumors would spread fast throughout Upland, and in no time the entire Green Isles would know about the twins.

"Robert!" August looked startled when he saw Robert coming out of his house.

"What? You thought I might not be home because I should be at work at this hour? And that you'd just pop in and see my wife?" Robert's face was a deep red shade.

August chuckled uneasily. "Where have you been for the past few months? I heard you and Desiree were over on the continent. Were you in La Belle Terre?"

Lord Robert refused to tell him where they really were. Robert had a place in La Belle Terre that the public knew about, but four years back he had purchased his villa in Vinosa, under a pseudonym, because he wanted a private place to getaway. "We were celebrating a long, enjoyable honeymoon in the glorious sun," Lord Robert said.

"Well, you are wrong about assuming I came here to see Desiree. I'm here to speak with you, actually. About your brother. Leo lost ten thousand more pins to me. And he still owes me forty thousand from the last time he lost to me. He says he has no money, and I should talk to you about it."

Robert grinded his teeth, but before he could respond, Desiree came out front. Lord Wellington immediately rushed over to her and grabbed her hands to kiss them.

"Desi. It has been a long time since I saw you. You look more radiant than ever. You're absolutely glowing." He kissed her hands and let his lips linger on them.

Acid boiled in Lord Robert's abdomen. He wondered why Lord August would use that term, "glowing." Was it a hint that he knew Desiree had been pregnant? Did he somehow find out about the twins?

Lord August went on, "You know, I just spoke with Dillon, your old friend and film director, Desi. He was asking me about you. He said there is a role in his next film that he thinks you'd be perfect for."

"Really? Oh, I do miss acting." Desiree glanced at Robert. "You're not going to mind if I decide to act again, are you, my love?"

"Of course, I won't mind. You are free to do as you choose." Robert didn't like that Wellington was still holding his wife's hands, and standing far too close to her.

"Good, I'll let Dillon know you are interested," he said, looking into her eyes. He reminded Robert of a vampire. "There is a reading tomorrow. You should go," Wellington was now closing the distance between himself and Desiree.

"I should love that," she said breathlessly. Robert wanted to run at August and grab him by the throat. It took all his strength to hold himself back. Instead, he walked to Desiree and pulled her back, away from August, wrapping an arm tight around her waist.

"I should love to see you act again, my love," Robert said, kissing her on the cheek. She beamed, as she looked up at him.

August's pale face hardened into a cold stone, as he said in a whispery voice, "Robert, you can send the fifty thousand pins you owe me tomorrow." August's expression changed as he looked once again into Desiree's eyes. He smiled, and again a vampire came to Robert's mind. "With Desiree. I'll be at the reading. I look forward to seeing you there, my dear."

He got into his flashy sports car and drove off.

"Pff. Don't you dare pay him a dime, Robert," Desiree said.

"I wasn't planning on it. Desiree, I'm happy you want to act again. But why is *he* going to be at the reading tomorrow? Is he going to be in this film with you?"

"I have no idea. He's a terrible actor. Dillon wouldn't give him anything more than a bit part. But oh, Robert! Dillon is a brilliant director! He directed *The Mermaid*. He's the absolute best of the best and I love working with him! I have to see what role he wants me to play," Desiree said.

To tell her she couldn't go would have provoked her to resent him, and she was certain to do whatever she wanted anyway, despite what Robert had to say about it. That was Desiree. Still, he was eaten up at the thought of her seeing Lord August again. As she was getting ready the next morning, he said, "Let me go with you. I don't trust Wellington."

"Honestly, Robert." Desiree was angry with him. "You're acting like a control-freak. We'll be around other people all day; it isn't like Wellington can hurt me. Plus, those bodyguards you hired to watch me will be there too, remember? They follow me everywhere I go outside of this house."

"He'd better not get near you." Robert clenched his jaw and stopped himself from saying anything else about it.

"Quit worrying so much. I'll be fine." She kissed him quickly before she was off to the reading.

Desiree came home later than she had promised. Her breasts were painfully engorged with milk, and the first thing she did after coming through the doors was rush upstairs to feed the babies. While she sat in one of the nursery rocking chairs feeding Elizabeth, who was always the plumpest, loudest, and most demanding twin, Lord Robert followed his wife with Luke in his arms. He grabbed a bottle of pumped milk and fed his son in the other rocker.

"Why did the reading take so long? You said it would be three hours," Robert kept his voice low for the sake of his babies.

"Oh, Robert, please," Desiree rolled her eyes, annoyed with his persistent badgering. "Dillon had me reading with several people. He was trying out parts, seeing if they had chemistry. But my milk came in, and oh! I was so engorged, I actually had to leave before everyone else."

Lord Robert said nothing more about it. He knew how to read people, and he saw how annoyed she was with him for questioning her. Simon had told Robert once, back when he was training, that acting was Desiree's first love. More important to her than anything. If that was true, then he and the twins came in second place. He sat there in silence, internalizing all that was going through his mind, as Desiree switched babies, and fed Luke awhile, while he held his baby girl, Elizabeth.

He looked over at Desiree, as she fed his son, and watched her drift off to sleep with the infant at her breast. He became overwhelmed by how beautiful she was.

After Luke finished eating, Desiree opened her eyes and said, "Oh my, it just zaps me of all my energy to feed these little monsters." She stood to walk Luke over to his crib. "I'm exhausted. Afraid I'm going to bed early tonight, Robert." Lord Robert put Elizabeth in her crib and pulled Desiree into his arms.

"Goodnight, my love. No doubt you'll be amazing in your new film," Lord Robert whispered, then kissed her passionately, hoping he might tempt her to stay awake long enough to make love to him.

"Mmm. Goodnight," she smiled up at him before she disappeared out the door, and left him looking after her. Frustrated. Yearning for her. Jealousy once again reared its ugly head.

Lord Robert tried to push out the thoughts that were forcing their way into his mind. Did she really ever love him? Or was she secretly in love with August? The thoughts grew louder. What if she chose to leave him? Leave the babies? It took two years to film *The Mermaid*. What if this film took her away from them for two years? How would he live two years without her? He couldn't imagine living two weeks without her.

She'd once told him that marriages never worked for actors.

Stop these maddening thoughts, he said to himself.

Robert walked down the hall and knocked on the nurse maid's door, which was slightly opened. The elderly maid was sitting at her desk inside, knitting.

"Peggy," he said, "Desiree is exhausted. Do you mind starting your shift a little early? The babies are sleeping but if you can listen for them in the monitor, would you? I'll be downstairs working in my study."

He headed down to his study. The daily maid and the butler were off duty that night, and the house was far too quiet. Robert's maddening thoughts persisted.

"What if I just go up there and start making love to her? Show her I'm number one. Show her no one can love her the way I do?" It had been over a week since they'd been intimate, and he was going insane.

"No. She is exhausted. That's all it is. She isn't rejecting me. She's not in love with August. Or Dillon. Or anyone else." He went into the ballroom, where he trained, and pulled a sabre off the wall. He needed to do something to get the crazy, screaming thoughts out of his mind. Exercise, martial arts, fencing... this was the way Robert handled stress. He loaded up his favorite playlist for working out, songs with sixteenth-note bass lines, screaming distorted guitars, and hard-hitting, fast-paced drums that were loud in the mix. Music that would chase out all the crazy thoughts in his head and help him focus on his workout. Fortunately, the ballroom was sound-proofed, so the babies and Desiree wouldn't be awakened.

About three hours later, Robert turned off his music. He heard the babies crying upstairs. "Surely Peggy has it covered," he thought, sweat dripping off of him.

A few minutes went by, and a blood curdling scream came from upstairs. He ran up to see what was going on. Peggy was in the hall, frozen, staring, covering her mouth with both hands. When she saw Robert, she ran into his arms, sobbing.

"What's wrong?" He asked, worried about his twins.

"I-I w-was just..." The maid shook and sobbed uncontrollably.

Robert released Peggy and ran to the nursery, where the babies were both now beside themselves because they'd been left crying for longer than they were used to.

"No! No! It's not the babies!" Peggy cried, and pointed down the hall to Desiree's room. She rocked herself back and forth. "It's your wife!"

"What's wrong with my wife? What are you saying? What's wrong with Desiree?"

The maid was hysterical at that point, saying things in her native language, which Robert couldn't understand. He ran into the outer part of Desiree's room, where there was a sitting area. He walked through it, and entered the inner chamber of the Master Bedroom, where the four-poster bed was, and where Desiree had been sleeping.

What he saw on the floor in front of him caused him to stumble backwards, winded.

First, an isolated, bloodied hand. Then, a chopped off foot.

He looked at the body on the bed. His wife. His Desiree.

The love of his life had been mutilated in the bed. Pieces of her body cut out, eyeballs missing from the sockets.

A word had been cut into her soft cheek. "Whore."

Tunnel vision set in, and Lord Robert lost his balance. He sucked air, only to feel even more suffocated. "No. No. Why? How- how could anyone...?" It made no sense to him, the diabolic nature of it.

Lord Robert wasn't thinking straight when he ran to her bedside and tried to put her hand back where it belonged, as if he could fix what had been broken. He picked up her dismembered foot and placed it where it belonged. "Her eyes... where are her eyes? I'm sorry, my love. So sorry, my perfect angel, my beautiful..." Lord Robert collapsed.

The Upland House was filled with cries and waling, coming from the babies in the nursery. But there was nobody home in their right mind to give them comfort. Peggy, the nurse maid, was unable to calm down. Lord Robert sat still, paralyzed. "I'm so sorry," he repeat. Over and over.

When the press got word of the news of Desiree's murder, rumors began to spread throughout The Greens, and travelled as far as Zone B.

COURTNEY

PRESENT

Courtney's House, Mill Pond

"Did you hear about that lord-guy who killed his wife?" My mom and me spoke almost every day on the phone. She and my father became tired of the dark, rainy winters in Cascadia, and decided to move back to The Goldens after I graduated high school. My mom always seemed to know the latest juicy gossip that was going around.

"What lord-guy, Mom?" I asked, not having a clue what she was talking about.

"Oh, I don't know his name. Some lord-something or other. It was all over social media. He chopped pieces of her body out. So disgusting.

I guess he got away with it. Probably paid off the judge, like rich people always do."

"Hmm." I had no idea. Spending time on social media was torture to me. I had a million things to do, two active kids to raise, ten wooded acres to excavate, a garden to weed, animals to feed. But my mom, she had just turned eighty, and had absolutely nothing better to do than look at social media all day.

"Is this some guy on television or something?" I asked her, thinking she was talking about an actor.

"Oh no. He's a real lord over in The Greens," she explained.

"Really? I don't follow the royal families in The Greens, or anywhere else over there in Zone A, Mom. Heck, I don't even follow what goes on in my own Zone."

"Well, you should watch the news more often. If that volcano by you is about to go off, you won't have a clue. Everybody around you will be evacuating and you'll be doing whatever it is you do out there in the middle of those woods, getting swept away by a river of lava."

My mom resented me for living so far away from her and this was how she expressed her resentment. By imagining me dying in a volcanic eruption.

"Well, at least I have you to fill me in on what is happening with the royals over in The Greens, and no doubt I can count on you to send me a text if the volcano is going to erupt. I'm sure you'll know it's going to happen way before anyone else does, Mom."

"Sure. But you probably won't check your text in time because you'll leave your phone in the car, like you always do."

"You're always right, Mom. Always right."

Keith came in the room and spoke loud enough for my mom to hear him over the phone. "Yep, that's what I always say. Your mom is always right, Courtney."

"Hi Keith," my mom said. "Flattery will get you nowhere. Bring my daughter and grandkids here to visit me if you want to stay on my good side."

That viscount my mom was talking about that day was the one and the same Lord Robert Ranfurly who I would one day meet. It is ironic, to think that Desiree's death, horrific as it was, brought Lord Robert and I together, in a round about way. Had she not died, had Lord Robert not been suspect in her death, he most likely would have no reason to move to Cascadia and I would have never met him.

✦— ▸ 12 ◂ —✦

LORD ROBERT

PRESENT
Upland House

So far Lord Robert had kept the press from learning about the twins. But he knew it would be impossible to keep his babies a secret forever.

A couple of days following the murder, Robert was sitting in his study, unable to focus on work, staring out the window. A light knock on the closed doors interrupted him.

"Come in," Robert said.

It was the maid who had been off duty the night of Desiree's murder. "I'm sorry, sir, but I'm putting in my notice."

"Oh. This is unexpected." Robert felt numb, out of body. "May I ask why?"

She avoided his questioning eyes. "I have a family situation I need to take care of back home in Vinosa."

"I'm sorry to hear that. You'll be missed around here."

The following day, the butler put in his resignation. He, too, had a reason to return to Vinosa and would not look Robert in the eye.

The only staff left was the nurse maid, Peggy. Minutes after the butler resigned and walked out the front door, old Peggy bustled into the study where Robert was getting nothing done, and blurted, "They all think you did it!"

"What?" Lord Robert looked at her, bewildered. "What do you mean? They think I did what?"

"They think you killed her, my lord!" Peggy cried, and hurriedly explained. "But I know you couldn't have. I peeked in and saw you doing your fencing training, then headed upstairs. When I was at the top of the stairs, I heard a noise in Desiree's room, and thought it was her waking up. So, I went in to see if she wanted her babies brought to her." Pause. "And I... found her... like that." She started to cry. "There was someone else was in the house. I know it!"

"It's alright, Peggy." Lord Robert got up and wrapped his strong arms around the frail, old maid. She reminded him of the nanny who had raised him as a child. "I can't believe my own staff thinks so terrible of me," he said, looking out the window. "What kind of person must I come across as to everyone? How do they not know I loved Desiree more than life itself?"

"I know you did, my lord. I know." Peggy said, patting him on his neck in a motherly way. She broke free of his embrace and said, "Oh, that reminds me. I found this in the drawer next to Desiree's dresser. It was her Scriptures. I thought you would want to keep it close to your heart. Before she died, she was a devoted soul, she was. I saw her reading the Scriptures every night. Often, she'd start weeping. Dear, dear soul.

No doubt, she's with the good Creator now, under His mighty wing. Waiting for you."

"Thank you Peggy," Lord Robert said.

He wasn't religious, and he never imagined Desiree would be the religious type either. But he had noticed a change in her when she was seven months pregnant, when they were living in Vinosa. She started going to a weekly prayer meeting in their little village. He thought it was a strange phase and attributed it to hormones.

Robert took his wife's Scriptures up to his room and flipped it open. Her small, elegant handwriting caught his eye. He traced his finger over the ink.

Verses were highlighted and circled. In the margin, Desiree's had written, *Grace. Forgive me.*

"What in God's name could she have wanted to be forgiven for? And who is Grace?" Robert decided he would look through her Scriptures and see if he could discover more. The next thing she wrote that caught his eye was, *Light exposes the darkness. Robert.*

"My name? Why did she write my name? What did she mean by that?"

As he continued to search through her Scriptures, the police came to his door.

"Lord Robert Ranfurly. We have some questions to ask you about the murder of your wife, Desiree Ranfurly."

Robert was gripped with fear, mixed with anger, frustration. Why were the police wanting to ask him questions? The way they looked at him, it was as if he were a suspect. "Yes?"

"Your fingerprints were the only ones found in the room on your wife's corpse. In addition to that evidence, two people who once worked for you testified that they'd seen you coming out of your wife's room just after the murder."

"What? They're lying. They were both off duty that night. They weren't even here!"

"One of them says they came back and saw you in your ballroom, claims you were in a frenzy, waving around your sabre like a maniac, an hour before your wife was found chopped up. The other one said they were coming home and saw you drive away on your motorcycle," one of the officers said.

"Looks like the evidence is stacked against you," the other officer said, clearly convinced Lord Robert was guilty. The police arrested him, threw him in prison until his trial date, and for the six months that followed, he was plunged into a nightmare.

As Robert was cuffed and taken away in a patrol car, he called back to Peggy. "Peggy...the children..."

"Don't worry, Lord Robert. You can count on me!" Peggy called to him, tears streaming down her cheeks.

For the first time in his life, Robert couldn't think of a solution. He had no way to fix this problem. He'd be looking at a life sentence if he was found guilty, and the worst art of it all, he was being separated from his babies.

The months passed, and the case against him was indeed a difficult one to fight. Just when it seemed like it couldn't get worse, some false witness would take the stand.

The only light in the midst of it all was Peggy, who visited him often and filled him in on how the babies were. She told him she'd made up a story that the twins were her grandchildren who she was taking care of until their parents returned from a long trip.

The day before his verdict would be determined, his attorney spoke with him.

"Do you pray, Robert? If so, you might want to spend this night on your knees. It doesn't look good," his attorney said.

"Those aren't the words a person hopes to hear from their attorney the day before their sentence is to be decided."

"Look, I did my best. But it seems that if you are innocent, someone has it out for you. The witnesses, this case. It's stacked against you. Some things in life are out of our human control, and we need divine intervention," his attorney said.

"Has Peggy taken the stand?" Robert asked.

"Early on she did, but she was a terrible witness. Cried the whole time. Didn't make a lot of sense, spoke a lot of words in her native language."

"Is there nothing else you can do?" Robert asked.

"As I told you, I'm out of all options. We need a divine hand at play now. If you're found guilty, you can be sure it'll be Death by Execution. "

For the first time in his life, Robert resorted to prayer.

When he went into the courtroom the next day, he looked over at the six witnesses, wondering what they had decided. He was sure by the look on their faces they were going to rule he was guilty.

But then he noticed the judge. It was a different judge than the one who had been residing over his case. A judge he had never met, and he was a lawyer. He'd met almost all the judges in Upland.

Next, he noticed Peter Williams in the observer section. The last time he'd seen Peter, he'd been angry at him and Nina for speaking ill about Desiree. What was Peter doing here?

Lord Robert was led to his seat, and the judge hammered his gavel on the podium. "Order in the court!" he said and after the room quieted, he continued. "The judge who was assigned to this case suffered a severe heart attack last night and is in the hospital. It is not certain whether he will survive. I have been assigned to take over, and have been filled in on all of the details of the case. I would like to ask the defendant's attorney, have you any more witnesses you would like to call at this time?"

"Yes, Your Honor. I have one more witness to call. Will Sophie Batiste please come to the stand?"

Robert was confused. *Sophie? She'd moved back to La Belle Terre, so how could she be a witness?*

"Sophie, do you recognize this man?" the attorney asked Sophie.

"Oui. I mean yes, Monsieur. I do know him. That is Lord Robert Ranfurly, Viscount of Knoxfordshire."

"How well do you know Lord Robert, Sophie?"

"I know him very well, Monsieur. He allowed me to live in his home for a couple of months, and he was the husband of my best friend, Desiree Diamond."

"You know him well, you say," the attorney continued. "Do you know him well enough to judge whether he seems like a man who would murder his own wife?" The attorney looked at the jury. "His wife who was *your* best friend."

"I do know him very well, and no. No, he is not the kind of person who would do that. He is a very good man. Also, I am certain he did not kill Desiree," Sophie said.

"You're certain, you say?" The attorney looked at the jury, then back at Sophie. "Certain is an absolute, Ms. Batiste. How can you be certain Lord Robert is not the murderer of his wife?"

"I was in the house that night. Visiting Desiree, before she died."

You could cut through the thick tension with a blade in the courtroom. The look on the faces of everyone was unblemished shock. Jurors, observers, and the prosecution team alike were all struck dumbfounded.

"Yes, I was back in Upland, and I stopped by. The first thing I saw that I thought a bit odd was a motorcycle. It was not parked on the driveway, but it was at the side of the house, on the grass. It wasn't Lord Robert's motorcycle because it was a different make and model. Lord Robert rides a Kingston Thoroughbred. But the bike I saw was a Fleetwood Thrasher."

"I see," said the attorney. "Make a note of that," he said to the jurors. "The motorbike's make and model. This counters the accusation of a witness who claims they saw Lord Robert on his motorcycle leaving the house. Please continue your testimony, Ms. Batiste."

Sophie went on. "I still had a key, so I let myself into the front door. I'd seen the lights were on in the ballroom windows, so I peeked in. Lord Robert was there, doing his workout, so I decided not to disturb him. It was a routine for him, practicing his fencing with foil and sabre, playing his loud music." She laughed. "Nothing out of ordinary."

"Jurors, make a note of that, as well. The maid claimed she'd seen Robert acting wild with a sabre. This testimony sheds a light on that claim quite a bit, doesn't it?" The attorney turned back to Sophie. "Go on, Ms. Batiste."

"Then I went up to Desiree's bedroom and woke her up. She'd been napping, and was happy to see me. It had been a long time since we saw each other. We spent a good hour talking before I left. I peeked in on Lord Robert on my way down, thinking I might say goodbye. But I saw he was still working out."

"What time did you leave, Ms. Batiste?"

"It was ten o'clock p.m. I remember looking at my watch as I got in my car."

"And Peggy claims Lord Robert came upstairs and found his wife at five minutes past ten," the lawyer said. "It is a large home, isn't it, Ms. Batiste?"

"Very large, yes."

"How long does it normally take you to get from Desiree's bedroom to the ballroom downstairs?"

"Normally, about five minutes. But I stopped in my old room and grabbed a few things I'd left behind when I'd moved out before I went down to peek in on Lord Robert," Sophie explained.

"Ah. So, let me see if I'm understanding you correctly. You saw an unfamiliar motorbike parked in an odd location on the premise before you went into the house. You saw Lord Robert doing a routine workout upon your arrival. You saw Desiree alive before you left. And what time did you leave Desiree's room?"

"I am not certain, but it only took me about ten minutes to stop in my room before I left. I thought the house seemed empty, too. It was so quiet, except for when I peeked in on Lord Robert."

"And you checked in on him again in the ballroom, before you left at ten?"

"Yes, and he was still doing his routine. No blood stains on his knives, no sign of blood anywhere. I know he did not kill her. Someone else was in the house when I was there. And whoever that person was, they killed my best friend while I was still in the house. When I was in my old bedroom getting my things."

Sophie, who usually had perfect composure, broke down and began to cry.

"How do you know that, Ms. Batiste?"

Because as I was getting in my car, I saw someone get on the Thrasher motorcycle and ride off down the driveway, in a hurry."

"Did you get a good look at the person who rode off on the motorbike, Ms. Batiste?"

"No, I'm afraid I couldn't tell who they were. They wore a black helmet and a black leather riding outfit. But I didn't think they looked very tall. Lord Robert is much taller than this person was. I know whoever rode that motorcycle was the same person who brutally killed Desiree."

Sophie's testimony saved Robert from being convicted of murder.

But her testimony didn't change the fact that his reputation had been marred. Once he was ruled "not guilty", and he was free again to live a normal life, his life went back to being anything but normal. At work, he could hear the whispers of people who used to admire him.

"Did you hear that he paid people to get him off?" "Of course, we all know he killed her. She was sleeping with Lord Wellington, and he was jealous!" "Who knew that beneath such a perfect, handsome face was a brutal monster?"

Lord Robert decided Upland was not the best place to raise his twins. He needed to leave Upland House, go somewhere far away where nobody knew him.

Around that time, an unexpected door opened for Lord Robert. A letter came from the attorney of a cousin he'd never met.

To Lord Robert Alexander Ranfurly, III,

I am writing to inform you that you are the sole beneficiary of the will of Mr. Theodore Gerald Ranfurly, of North Ireland, Cascadia, Zone B. Due to the fact that Mr. Ranfurly has no other living relations, Ranfurly Manor and the thirty-thousand-acre estate it sits on have been transferred into your name. In addition, the entire household staff, every vehicle, airplane, furnishing, and all other items, land, and business in which Mr. Ranfurly possessed are now yours. Your signature on the agreement will make it official.

Before Mr. Theo Ranfurly passed, he confided in me, saying, "I've never met my cousin, Lord Robert. But last night, I was visited in a dream by a raven. It whispered his name to me, and I believe it was a clear sign that he's the one who should inherit my estate. May it serve him well, and may he serve it well."

The raven, the symbol on your family crest, has spoken.
Sincerely,

Mr. George Steinberg, Attorney at Law

"Hmm." Lord Robert twirled his model of the globe. "North Ireland, Cascadia. Let's see… there is Cascadia. But I must need to look at a close up of the region to find this North Ireland place. Must be a tiny village."

Cascadia was across the ocean, in Zone B. The largest city, Emer Aude, was globally known for its excellent seafood, beautiful mountains that surrounded it, and lush evergreens. Also, for having one of the highest percentages of drug and human trafficking on the globe.

"Let's see," Robert pulled up a map on his phone to see a close up of the region. "There it is. North Ireland. Population 109. Looks like there's nothing but forest surrounding it for miles and miles. But it's far enough away from Emer Aude. Probably a safe place to raise children."

Lord Robert needed an escape, and this sounded like the answer. If he didn't even know he had a cousin in Cascadia, then surely nobody else would know.

What's more, Ranfurly Manor was tucked far into the wilderness of Cascadia, and in a place like that Lord Robert was certain nobody would know who he was. He now had a place where he could disappear to with his twins. The only person he had to tell would be Roger, who handled his properties and business affairs. But Roger was trustworthy not to tell a soul.

And Peggy. He would need her to look after the twins who were about eight months old at that time.

Robert signed the agreement, hired a pilot, giving him pseudonyms for himself and the twins, along with a ton of money to keep quiet, and the four of them left The Greens far behind with no thought of when they might return.

Lord Robert's sudden disappearance caused many people to wonder whether he was dead or alive.

✦ — ➤ 13 ◄ — ✦

COURTNEY

FUTURE – YEAR 2227
In Flight

"Yes. You're going home to see mom?" One of the men in the dark suits was sitting behind me on the plane, talking on his phone. "Okay. Tell her I'll be home next week. Have to finish an assignment for work first."

It was strange to think the man actually had a mom. They were PAX thugs, but they were only human, after all.

My mother. She adored Keith. And he adored her.

FLASHBACK - THREE YEARS AGO
Courtney's House, Mill Pond

"Come on, Courtney-coo. Come with me this time. We can fly your mom up for ten days to help with the kids," Keith suggested.

I looked at him like he was crazy. "My mom?" I laughed and shook my head. "You still think of her as the same age she was when you met her, don't you?" I laughed. "She's eighty-two now, Keith. She wouldn't want to be a taxi driver for the kids for ten days."

He sighed. "Well then, I guess I'll just have to miss you. Again."

"Mmhmm," I said. "But at least we get to have fun making up for lost time when you get back." I gave him a teasing kiss.

"Stop torturing me, babe. You know I have to catch a flight." Keith kissed me on the cheek. "But I'm glad it is only ten days. Any longer would be too long without you." He gave my bottom a squeeze. "And this."

"You amaze me, Keith, the way you drop everything when there's a crisis. I'm so proud of you." I smacked him with one last, quick kiss. Then he was off to catch a plane, to go be a hero by helping victims of a hurricane. I sighed. That was my man.

As he did with every overseas trip, he texted me when he arrived, and checked in with me daily. But this time, after the fourth day of his trip I stopped hearing from him. I assumed it was a connection issue since he was in a different zone, The Tropics Zone. I waited every day, but never heard from him. As each day passed, I grew more worried and couldn't wait until he finally came home and was back in my arms.

The day his flight was due to arrive home, I anxiously waited for him at the airport. Keith's other team members had family waiting for them at the airport, as well. All of them had the same story as mine. They'd been unable to connect since the fourth day of their trip and were worried something might be wrong.

Our worst fears came true that day when their scheduled flight emptied of its passengers and Keith and his team weren't among them. At that point, we were all panicking. We reported the situation to the airlines and to our embassy over in The Tropics, but the embassy had no knowledge of Keith and his team's whereabouts.

What could have happened to them?

Before Keith left for his trip, a few things had happened in the world that seemed unrelated to his disappearance. I would one day discover that they were, in fact, related.

Just before the hurricane in The Tropics, a war broke out in the Sand Belt Region. The tribes in the Sand Belt often were at war, but this was a larger war, and one of the tribes had managed to get their hands on dangerous weapons that, if used, would be dangerous for the entire world.

Ten billionaires, globalists, who called themselves The Peace Alliance Ten, or PAX, had managed to stop the weapons from flying in that region by mastering the use of AI. The globalists looked like they might be able to solve some of our world's problems.

Nobody trusted the monarchies anymore in Zone A. The leaders in the Sand Belt and the Eastern zones were insane. Our zone was still a democracy, but the leaders who had been voted in were complete idiots. Good leadership was desperately needed in the world. So, when PAX stepped in, everyone embraced them.

But when the new government started to carry out punishments in their own way, came up with a whole new set of rules for people to follow, and designed a prison island where they sent those who broke their new laws, people like my husband didn't like what they saw.

Keith wasn't one to obey rules if he disagreed with them.

Then, after Keith's team disappeared, PAX announced that Cat 4 Prison had reached full capacity, and they were going to execute the prisoners to make room for new ones. They called it The Day of Cleansing. The event would be livestreamed for the world to see.

When the Day of Cleansing arrived, my son Nick, sixteen at the time, turned on our flatscreen to watch it. "Mom, I was thinking. What if Dad and his team got arrested and taken to that island?"

"Nick, that's crazy. The people PAX sent to the island are criminals."

Even as I denied it, my stomach twisted into knots, dreading that it could be true.

"Daddy was helping people, Nick! PAX didn't arrest him," My fifteen-year-old daughter, Laurel, said.

"Dad and his friends on that team were all pretty loud and opinionated about politics and made it no secret that they weren't fans of PAX. But PAX arrests people who speak out against them. What if Dad and his team shared their opinions when they were on that trip to The Tropics? Maybe a PAX worker overheard them and reported them."

"Nick, we shouldn't jump to conclusions like that. We can't give up hope that he is alive. He'll find his way back to us."

Nick insisted on watching the Day of Cleansing because he wanted to make sure his dad wasn't there. I had no desire to see it, and avoided the living room flatscreen, but at one point I had to walk through the living room to get to my bedroom, and I caught a glimpse of a scene; the camera showed a bird's eye view of drones dropping explosive bombs into a crater filled with thousands of people. I quickly looked away.

"Nick, why are you watching that?" I snapped at him. "You can't see the faces of people who are there. And your dad isn't there. I know he isn't." It was unsettling, hearing the cinematic music play behind the scenes. As if it were an episode of a film, and not reality. Even if those were criminals, it was demented to show them dying like that.

Nick's words plagued me, especially when I lay in bed at night, trying to fall asleep. Could Keith have been one of those hundreds of faces in the *trenches getting bombed? If he wasn't there, then where was he? Dead somewhere? Or alive, trying to find his way home to us?*

FUTURE – YEAR 2227

Site 205, Desert Region

Somehow, my memories had gone from pleasant to disturbing. I'd wanted to escape to a happy place... not to memories of losing Keith.

Okay, time to switch thoughts. Lord Robert... I'll let myself think of him now. The last time I saw him I was angry with him. But I want to remember the happiest moments with him. Only two short months ago we met, and he took my breath away. The most beautiful, intriguing man on the planet. The first and only man after Keith that I'd let into my heart. What I would give to see him again. To feel his kiss. To look into his eyes one more time...

The plane's wheels touched down and jerked me out of my thoughts, only to wake me up to the very unpleasant reality of a man's gun staring me in the face. Time to get off the plane.

The passenger door opened, and a blast of dry heat came over me. The Desert Region.

I hated any kind of heat, but worst of all, the dry kind. My head was beginning to throb and I could feel the blood vessels in my nose already threaten to bleed.

The Desert Region, the place where nothing grew in the sand except tumble weed and ugly cacti. *Joy.*

We descended the rolling staircase and were met at the bottom by a young woman in a hot pink lab coat. Hot pink. Kind of weird and out of place.

"Courtney Drake. Follow me." She was a beautiful young lady, around my son's age. Golden skin, innocent-looking eyes, round and blue, long copper-streaked hair that shimmered in the bright desert sun. She had a little, happy skip to her step, almost like a child. She certainly didn't look like anyone who belonged there, working at Site 205. The men with the guns pointing at me at all times, on the other hand, now they did a fine job looking menacing.

"Those guns won't be necessary here. She can't exactly escape now, can she?" the woman said to the men, gesturing to the barren desert around us. She was right. There was nowhere to run. "Also, she won't be needing this." She quickly ripped the duct tape off my mouth.

""Ow!" I yelled.

"Sorry. That probably felt worse than a lip wax." She made a face, her mouth formed into a rectangle showing a healthy overbite. She looked sincerely empathetic as she handed me a bottle of water. "It isn't poisoned, I promise."

I didn't care if it was, I was dying of thirst. I took a swig of water, while the men put their guns back in holsters, and we followed the woman into a cave cut into the side of rock. Inside the mouth of the cave the woman put her thumb print on a finger scanner and the cave wall opened. We stepped in, and she put her eye up to a retina scanner.

Her scanned eyeball granted us access to an elevator. We stepped inside it, and the elevator doors closed us in. I could feel pressure in my ears as the elevator descended.

Down, down, down.

About the Author

From the time she was a teenager, K.M. Krenik spent much of her energy writing songs, journals, and plays. Her first published writings are under the name Kim Krenik: a cookbook called *Family Favorites Recipes* which includes stories and recipes passed down by her Italian grandmother and other family members; and a women's bible study called *Fire Lilies – Out of the Ashes*.

As a reader, K.M. has been a longtime fan of mystery novels, clean romance novels, and fantasy stories. *The Ranfurly Mysteries* series blends of all her favorite genres. She hopes readers will delight in it as much as she delights in bringing the story to life.

K.M. lives in the lush and lovely Pacific Northwest with her family, where they are learning how to homestead on thirty acres. When the sun comes out in her neck of the woods, she enjoys excavating, gardening, hiking on the hunt for waterfalls, and kayaking.

Who murdered Desiree Diamond?

What happened to Keith Drake?

What will happen to Courtney at Site 205?

The mysteries begin to unravel in **Danger Lies Within**
The Ranfurly Mysteries Book One
by K.M. Krenik

www.kmkrenikbooks.com

The Old Map with Languages

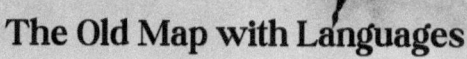

The Green Isles: Uplandish   Gutland: Gutish   Tsur: Tsurish

Highland: Highlandish   Vinosa: Vinosian   The Northlands: Norrian

Chantelle: Chantellian   Felizia: Felizian   Loong Islands: Loongese

La Belle Terre: Bellaise   Sollam and Qud: Sollamish   Ortus: Ortese

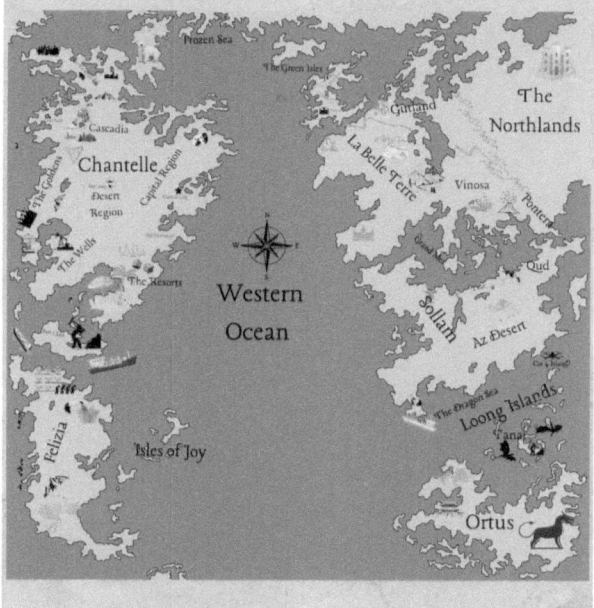

www.ingramcontent.com/pod-product-compliance
Lightning Source LLC
Chambersburg PA
CBHW051846170626
46807CB00003B/1373